the Teacher & the Soul

To Debbie

Love Diane

DIANE DUPUY

Beyond
Blacklight

Library and Archives Canada Cataloguing in Publication

Dupuy, Diane
      The teacher & the soul / Diane Dupuy; editor, Fina Scroppo; illustrator, Cal Courtney.

ISBN 0-9730736-3-2

      I. Scroppo, Fina II. Title III. Title: Teacher and the soul.

PS8557.U6768J68 2006   C813'.6   C2006-901979-7

Editor: Fina Scroppo
Copyeditor: Suzanne Moutis
Cover and Text Illustrations: Cal Courtney, www.calcourtney.com
Cover Design, Page Layout & Print Production: Beth Crane,
      Heidy Lawrance Associates, www.hlacreative.com

All inquiries should be addressed to:
Beyond Blacklight Inc.
33 Lisgar St.
Toronto, ON M6J 3T3
416-532-1137; Fax: 416-532-6945
Toll-free: 1-888-453-3385
Websites: www.beyondblacklight.com
      www.fpp.org

10 09 08 07 06   1 2 3 4 5

Printed and bound in Canada

This book has been printed on 50% post-consumer recycled paper,
with vegetable-based ink.

For our children and the
wounded child in all of us.

"You are not a grown-up
unless you grow up to be kind."

— Diane Dupuy

Acknowledgments

This is my third book edited by Fina Scroppo. Fina is like a fitness guru who pushes and pushes until you get into shape and lose weight to give you a complete makeover. Editing is like cutting the fat and giving you a nip and tuck at the same time. You hate the process, but when you see the final results you say, WOW! Fina you are the best. Thank you for your dedication to a story that is dear to my heart and I know yours too.

Special thanks to my personal assistants Yvonne Ibay Nichols and Brittany Knight.

Also, a special thanks to my angel Courtney, who flew into my life and put my imagination on paper through her angelic drawings.

This book belongs to

_____

A gift from

_____

CHAPTER ONE

A Teacher Is Born

*W*ho is this? I looked up at the most radiant face I had ever seen in my life. It seemed so transparent that I needed to get closer to it so I could see who it was. The light that was shining behind it was so bright and comforting that I wanted to live in its rays forever.

And where was I? I looked around me, but all I could see was light engulfing me. The light seemed to go on and on forever. I started to follow it to its source; the more I followed it, the more I could hear my thoughts being answered.

"You have come home," a voice said. Home? Where was home? If this was home why did I ever leave it? Is this Heaven? I glanced around me, looking to find the soft voice that was guiding me. The shape of a face was so illuminating that I could feel a presence of love bathing me like a warm shower.

Suddenly, I began to float high up in the sky to the point where I could no longer see the ground. Why don't I feel hungry and weak. I was breathing. I was alive! But I was alive in a different way. I looked down at my feet and I only saw light beneath me, as if I was sitting on a cloud. I felt like an angel.

I heard a voice whisper to me. "Now it is time for you to go back and share what you have learned."

"Go back where? I don't know where I am *now*."

"You're here with me, God, in Heaven, and you are Autumn."

"Autumn? That's not my name." But I couldn't think of my real name. Nor could I remember how I got here, even though I tried so hard.

"You lived only until you were 38 years old. Now, you have to go back to Earth, only this time as an angel," God spoke assertively to me. I stood before God, now a woman whose face was etched with lines from the difficult road I had traveled, much like a palm print that reveals the future. As God's light beamed down on me, my once tangled, graying hair unraveled and turned to silver in the breeze.

"Will I always feel this way—light and wonderful?"

"Not always," the voice spoke to me with empathy.

"You will be a teacher."

"A teacher? Why a teacher?" I asked.

"A teacher that will help a young boy named Rainbow."

"Where is he?"

"He has just been born and you will guide him in his life, just as your angel, Summer, guided you," he whispered.

"Summer, where is she now?" I asked. "And if she was guiding me, why didn't she guide me in the right direction in life?"

"Life on Earth is all about choice," said God's voice calmly. "That is why I created free will for all mankind. The journey in the end is entirely up to you."

Like a magic wand, God's breath sent a ray of colorful sparkles swirling around me, creating long wings that poked out from my shoulders. The light from God's face was still shining brightly and all I could see was a long glowing hand as delicate as silk chiffon reaching out to touch my shoulder. "You must remember: you should not, under any circumstances, try to control Rainbow or prevent him from making mistakes throughout his life. The choice is up to him and only him."

"I thought angels were always there to protect and guide people?" I was still confused about my role, but I couldn't help and open my arms wide to embrace God's glow.

"They do, only if the person chooses to listen and ask for help in the form of prayer or meditation. The choice is always up to the individual. NOT you!" God's voice sounded like thunder.

"I don't know how to be an angel," I admitted to God. "How did I get to Heaven? I've made so many mistakes. I took so many wrong paths and wasted my life. I destroyed and hurt the few friends and family I had. I'm ashamed at how I treated my body, the places I lived, and the terrible things I did just to survive. I'm not worthy of being an angel for this little boy. What do I do? Do I fly and pick him up and carry him away from danger and guide him in the direction he needs to go?"

"You can't fly," God replied.

"Why give me wings if I can't fly?"

"Trust in my plan and the answer will come to you."

"Then if I can't fly, how do I carry him away from danger?" I asked.

"Speak directly to him through his heart," God's voice now sounded so peaceful. I felt like I was a baby being rocked in his arms.

"He will hear you, only if he chooses to," God continued.

"Can he see me?" I asked.

"Only when he is born will he hear and see you, but then his memory of you will disappear as time goes on. Your presence is what he will continue to feel, but only if he chooses to."

"Okay, but how will I know what to do when he gets into trouble if he can't see or hear me?"

"You need to know only one thing," God reassured me. "You are the boy's spiritual teacher. Everyone has an angel assigned to them, and like all the other angels, what you need to do will come to you and it is then that you will remember from past experiences what wisdom he will need to hear from you."

The light got even stronger then I could ever imagine. I felt God kissing me goodbye as he wrapped me with love in a feathered cloak and blew to me golden stars that turned into a locket. "What is this for?" I asked him.

"It's the boy's dream and it'll be kept safely in this locket. Take the locket, kiss it and direct it to his heart, and the rest is up to him," said the light.

"Can I look to see what's inside, so I know how to guide him?"

"Only the boy is allowed to look inside the locket. His dream is not your concern—that is between him and me. He can waste it or do something good with it. The choice is up to him! As for you, Autumn, remember you are a teacher and a teacher's job is to teach, but you should never stop learning."

Deep inside of me, I felt like I hadn't deserved to be Rainbow's spiritual guide. But I was ready for the challenge. I wanted so desperately to see if I could make amends for some of my own mistakes in life.

"NOW GO!"

CHAPTER TWO

Meeting the Soul

*O*uch! Bam! Pow! Oops!

The light, where's the light? Where was I? I heard thunder roll across the sky.

I dusted myself off, cursing under my breath. "God you didn't tell me I would have such a rough landing." I stood up and entered the doors of a hospital. It was starting to come back to me—the smell of the corridors, the blue gowns, and the people who were running around in a panic as I walked past the emergency room. I saw a woman lying on a stretcher while a doctor pounded her chest with his fists to get her heart pumping again. That was why this place was familiar to me. This was where I died. Next to her was her angel holding her hand. I wondered if she could feel her angel's touch, like I did when Summer held my hand before I took my last breath.

As I walked toward the maternity ward, I saw the nursery with all the newborn babies. I started to fly magically to get a bird's-eye view of all the special gifts God delivered. They were all lined up in a row, with angels beside them that looked like me, each holding a locket. Finally, I found the bassinet with Rainbow's name on it. He was beautiful; everything I imagined he would be. I took the locket God gave me and kissed it, just like God told me to do. Then it glowed, and like a shooting star, it disappeared into his heart.

"Rainbow, can you hear me?"

His eyes opened and he gazed at me. I knew he could see me. He gurgled, as if he was expecting my arrival.

⁓⚭⁓

In the months that followed, while Rainbow lay in his crib, I would put my head down near him and talked to him. When his mother came to pick him up and burp him over her shoulder, his head rolled over to look right at me.

"I'm here with you forever," I said.

He nodded his head and then he drooled all over my feathered coat as I lay next to him. "My name is Autumn and I'm your angel. I'm here to guide you on the right path in life, to help you make your dream come true."

He looked at me with the widest eyes I had ever seen. I thought about what I needed to say to him and tried to figure out how I was going to explain to this baby what a path was and how we can make mistakes and take the wrong path if we aren't careful, or take the right path that was meant to be just for us. Slowly and carefully, I put my words together to deliver my message. Tears of shame dripped down my face. How could I be trusted by God to send the right message to this innocent soul when I didn't even listen to Summer during all the many times she tirelessly tried to inspire me with the right choices to make?

At nighttime when Rainbow's mother put him down to sleep, I sat by Rainbow's crib and told him about our impending journey together and that his life was not going to be easy all the time. "You have this locket that's inside your heart and it holds your dream, waiting for you to discover it," I said to him.

Then my memory started coming back and I recalled the very words that Summer had once whispered to me. "Life is like climbing a giant magical mountain that will have you leaping, tripping, hanging from cliffs, falling off and struggling to get back on. Life is also about dreams. Making a dream come true is like climbing a mountain. We are like mountain climbers who dream of reaching the highest peak. However, in order to do so, you'll need to make the right choices. This is the same for anyone who wants to achieve something great and make their dreams come true. You will never get anywhere in life unless you make a commitment first," she would say over and over to me. "The payoff for making the right choices is great, including fulfillment, respect for yourself and others, good grades in school and eventually a good job," Summer encouraged me all the time.

As Rainbow reached out to touch my face with his soft tiny hands, I kept talking quietly as if I was singing a lullaby. "From the time you are born, Rainbow, life will always present you with obstacles. These obstacles are like giant boulders that block the path as you work your way up your mountain of knowledge and growth. Or the obstacles could be blocking your entrance to a path of destruction, giving you the opportunity to make a positive choice and take another path up the Mountain of Joy. The choice is up to you!

"Dream makers are no different than a mountain climber who is constantly challenged by giant obstacles and must figure out a way to overcome them."

Rainbow let out a little cry that sounded like a beautiful chime. I watched him as he wriggled around and kicked his blanket off his feet. I wanted to give him even more information to reinforce what I was saying so he would remember my words when he faced danger. "In life you must stay focused and steer yourself away from temptation, or you could find yourself facing a sudden avalanche of trouble heading your way.

"Life is filled with wonderful experiences too—like the great friends you'll make and the fun you'll have together. Or the sense of fulfillment and boost of confidence you'll get from riding your bike after months of practice. You should always remember the great things you'll achieve when you reach for the highest goals.

"So, how do you remain dedicated and focused on your goal?" I smiled at his beautiful blue eyes that sleepily opened and closed around his feeding times. "You have to learn to believe in yourself and remember that you have a dream in your heart that will never go away unless you let it."

Rainbow smiled at me throughout the night. I could tell he was overjoyed to hear me sing that the dream in his heart belonged only to him. I continued to tell him that with me by his side, he should not be afraid of life and the dangers that he may encounter, the enemies that he would meet, the people that he would befriend, the losses that he would endure and the rewards that he would receive.

"I will be with you every step of the way. I will whisper in your ear and give you a sign of warning and tell you the love I have for you every day. Sadly, there will be a time when you won't be able to hear or see me any longer."

Suddenly Rainbow belted out a sharp cry. His mother dashed in to lift him out of his bassinet and rock him quietly to sleep. To comfort him, I gently placed my soft pillowy hands beneath him, and wrapped my coat of feathers around him like his own security blanket.

As Rainbow fell in and out of his sleep throughout the night, I continued to remind him: "It's up to you. You will have the courage and trust in yourself to find the golden locket in your heart and to open it up to see what dream is inside. Like the sun bursting through a dark sky, your dream will appear. You can waste it or dedicate the rest of your life to making your dream come true. And when you do the latter, you will find that through one dream, a thousand more dreams unfold.

"The choice is up to you!"

CHAPTER THREE

Our Life Together

For the next few days, I continued to talk to Rainbow, embedding in his heart and mind very important things that God wanted him to know. I was to tell Rainbow that God had given him a beautiful imagination and he could use it in any way—good or bad. The choice was up to him.

"Imagine, Rainbow, that you have an invisible knapsack on your back. It holds all of your experiences and special tools that you will need as you begin to explore who you are. Once the knapsack is on, you can't take it off. It is there for *life*."

In the months that followed, I loved watching Rainbow as he crawled on the floor trying to find his way around the dining room table and chairs, exploring the world from the ground up. Everything and everyone appeared so big in Rainbow's eyes, yet he ventured fearlessly in his own surroundings.

A year went by and before I knew it Rainbow began to take his first steps. He would often fall down and then get back up and start all over again. I was glad to see his determination, a trait I knew would come in handy once he faced the world on his own. When he started to walk, he headed right toward me with eyes wide open and I knew that he could still see me.

We started to have lots of fun playing games together. I'd tickle his belly and he'd laugh and try to tickle mine. No matter how many new toys he received he always liked playing with the ones I helped him discover—the pots and pans under the sink. Bang! Bang! You could often hear as we drummed together on the pots on the linoleum floor. "Who is making all that noise? It sounds like there are two of you," Rainbow's mom would say as she looked over her shoulder from the sink. A new teddy bear replaced the noisy pots and pans; something that Rainbow could cuddle and love. His mother would tuck him into his crib with his teddy under his arm, but little did she realize that my head lay next to his.

Once he reached his terrible twos, Rainbow began to show a more boisterous personality, especially at the dinner table. Rainbow would often spit out his green peas, broccoli and meatballs, even though his mother did everything she could to get him to eat his food. She tried getting airplanes (the spoon) to land in his mouth or a choo choo train to pull into the station (his mouth), but Rainbow and I both knew the secret—it wasn't that he didn't like the food, rather that we both loved playing games with his mother who looked so silly with a spoon spinning in the air and green peas stuck in her hair! This was a time of fun and innocence when little ones, without realizing it, practice some basic skills and conquer huge challenges like talking, walking, building balance and coordination—the very same foundation that Rainbow would need in order to attain his dream. Watching Rainbow play filled me with excitement, but at the same time I felt a sense of fear buried underneath my joy, knowing full well that in the years to come, Rainbow would meet some real challenges, and if he chose the wrong road, the fun and games would be merely a memory in the far distance, almost a lifetime away.

Along with his devilish side, Rainbow still had a very sweet side. He loved to hug and kiss people and dolls. As he rocked on his horse, he often practiced saying new words. To everyone's delight, his first one was LOVE. "Luv, luv, luuv," you would often hear him rock back and forth to the beat of his love chant.

There was more fun at three and four. In fact, I called it his funny fours. His wavy blond hair with its uncontrollable curl hanging in the center of his forehead bounced up and down as we ran around the cherry tree playing games like Peekaboo, I See You and laughing.

He was slowly learning about life and its ups and downs, from riding a bike to learning the letters of the alphabet to practicing to tie his shoelaces. We sat under the fruit trees in his garden, where I taught him to take the pebbles on the ground or the petals from a flower and practice adding and subtracting. He was determined not to give up, and that was the strength I admired in him the most. His mother taught him how to get dressed and learn to tie his shoelaces. His dad taught him to play ball and play fair. Every Sunday, they visited friends with children and they showed Rainbow how to share his toys when playing with the other children.

One day while he was riding his tricycle on the sloped driveway huffing and puffing, he slipped, fell and scraped his knee. He yelled so loudly that his father came running from the garage to pick him up and give him a big hug along with some encouragement to keep trying. Little did he realize that I was sandwiched in between the two of them with my arms around Rainbow and his around me, my wings being flattened until a few feathers fell to the ground. This was another lesson in making choices—he could get back up on his bike and ride toward the future or sit out and let life pass him by. Encouraged by his father, he jumped back on the tricycle.

One early morning while Rainbow got up, I told him that before he begins his journey, he must know that everything in life happens for a reason.

"Why?" he asked.

"You'll need to learn about yourself and accept the weak traits along with good traits."

I told him that in order to achieve his dream, he couldn't give up on himself. You'll learn that your greatest successes can sometimes happen when you fail and face your failures. These experiences may even help you develop the depth of your character, build your stamina, prepare you for future experiences, and help you conquer your fears," I said.

"How will I learn all this?" he asked one day while he was riding his bicycle. "These experiences will be delivered to you by the many teachers that you will meet along the rocky road to the top of your mountain. Parents, grandparents, aunts, uncles and teachers will all help to guide you in the right direction in life, just like the signposts on a highway that guide us along the right route so we don't get lost. This can only be done when they lead you through their own examples—owning up to responsibilities, learning to forgive and, most importantly, becoming a person of honor and peace. Never forget to say your prayers and trust that your prayers will be answered in time. When you're in trouble, stay still and think of me, even though you won't be able to see me. I'll be there with you. Trust yourself and I will help guide you through your inner voice, if only you will listen."

Although Rainbow couldn't understand it yet, I reminded him that he could only hear me when he prayed or meditated, like his subconscious speaking to him. "But, I don't want you to go Autumn," he said.

"I'm not going. I will always be with you and you can speak to me through your heart and I will answer you," I explained to him. "Let me tell you about more lessons you need to learn before I leave." Rainbow listened as he sat on his bike.

"The road in which you travel will be full of interesting surprises. Each mountain will have hills, valleys, fields, bridges and glaciers to cross. Like a mountain climber, you will need to learn to find the right ledge on which to place your feet. If not, you will fall and experience unpleasant landings, just like when you fell off your bicycle earlier today. You were determined not to give up! You just got right back up and started to ride again. Life is just like that. In the end, through hard work and dedication, you will stand tall as you take your position on top of the highest mountain peak and wave your flag of victory.

"But for now, you'll begin at the bottom of your mountain, looking up high at the climb that awaits you."

"But the mountain is soooo tall," he said, as he stretched his neck up high to try and see the top of his mountain peak.

"Your walk may start off easy and picturesque, with many hills and valleys below. But as you go along, it becomes harder. Rain, snow, ice and wind will try to knock you down, or carry you forward."

"What do I do then?" Rainbow said with fear in his voice.

"That's where you find within yourself the tools of endurance that are in your invisible knapsack. Your endurance helps to push you forward. It is your stamina, your determination to never give up—no matter how hard, no matter how painful—that keeps pushing you forward to make your dream come true. Like the mountain climber, focus your sights on only one direction at a time as you look to reach your final destination."

☙

There were times when we played together that Rainbow's mother could see him talking to himself and she knew it was his 'invisible' friend named Autumn. She even went along with his imagination and packed a lunch for me when it was time for Rainbow to go to school. "It's just a phase he's going through," she said to one of her friends, and it broke my heart. I knew she was right. The time would soon come when Rainbow would take the journey of life by himself, and would only get my support and the support of those who loved him if he chose it. I would take his journey with him and hoped that he would listen to his heart, his inner voice, where he would find me.

On Rainbow's sixth birthday, I gave him a gift of more knowledge to carry with him on his journey when he could no longer hear or see me by his side. He listened intently to me. We sat on the branch of a tree, high above the meadow below. "Faith will become important during your climb in life—having faith in oneself and the power within," I told him. "To believe in one's dream and to know there is a place inside us where we can stop and quietly rest. It's the faith within you—your spirit—that can guide you toward your dream."

"You mean when I climb up my mountain I just have to remember to stop and take a rest and think before I rush ahead, and think about what I'm doing—good or bad?" said Rainbow, who was a very fast learner.

"Just remember life is all about choices," I said, "and know that the spirit inside of you is your soul."

"My soul?" He looked at me with great interest.

"God lives inside your soul and he lives in every teacher you will meet. He lives within the sky above you that becomes the universe that goes on forever, to a place we do not fully know. He lives in the clouds that change their shape, from rabbits to cowboys, and their color, from black to white.

"God is the man on the moon that looks like a round ice cube that melts when the sun, in all its glory, rises to take its place." Rainbow's eyes looked up to notice everything above him as I continued to speak. "He is the rapid river that flows powerfully, to the raindrops that fall softly to make the delicate flowers of every wondrous color grow.

"God is the tiny seed that becomes the acorn and then the tree, which cleans the air that we breathe. He is the Mother Earth that we walk on and every living creature no matter how small that takes their place on Earth. God is the breath inside you. If you look inward in silence, with the gentle touch of a prayer you will see God smiling back at you."

Rainbow leaned forward, smiled and waved back at God. We climbed down the tree from where we sat and started to walk back home to prepare for his first day of Grade 1—just one of the climbs up his magical mountain. I gave him a final reminder:

"Rainbow, when you need to make a choice or a decision on how to deal with a particular obstacle you face, be still and ask if this is good for you. Is this the right direction you are going in? When you do this, you are speaking directly to God and I'll help to answer your prayer. I will always be there with you, Rainbow, even when you can no longer see me."

Rainbow started to cry. "I don't want you to leave me," he said, now having a harder time hearing me. As I once told him as a baby, there would be a day when he could no longer see or hear me with such clarity. That day had come. I repeated myself as a tear rolled down my face.

I followed close behind as his mother and father took him by the hand and walked him to school, where he would enter a whole new world he didn't know existed. "Don't be afraid," his mother said, hugging him. "This is the place where you will meet new friends and learn how to paint, color, read and write." As his father picked him up in his big arms, he told him, "And at playtime, you'll even have other children to play ball with."

"Rainbow, always remember my coat made of feathers is there to shelter you and remind you of the love surrounding you," I was now standing behind his parents and yelling at him to be heard. "If a snowstorm sneaks up on you, my coat of feathers will protect you. Or my coat can turn into a soft pillow that you can throw up in the air when you are overcome with joy.

"When you're confused, take the time to pray or meditate. It'll calm you down and give you some head-space so you can figure out what to do next. This is the only way I can communicate with you."

Rainbow was having a hard time focusing on me as I faded, but I continued, hoping he could still hear me one final time. "The road you are traveling on is full of mystery, with many twists and turns and forks in it that you will face. When the road splits into different directions, you'll need to make a choice. Have trust in yourself and have faith in your climb as you try to reach the top of your personal mountain of dreams.

"Rainbow, Rainbow, can you hear me?"

Rainbow now looked past me and went on his way. I knew then he could no longer see or hear me.

CHAPTER FOUR

Rainbow's Magical Mountain

I looked up at the sky and yelled, "God you didn't tell me I would be back on Earth climbing a mountain again!" I saw myself in the past as a kid of 10—an awkward age when my legs were too tall and skinny for my body and I felt intimidated by the kids who came from families with money and who wore the latest fashions. It was the time I began to steal just so I could 'buy' my friendships. I felt sick recalling these bad times when I went into a store and grabbed as many chocolate bars as I could and shared them with all the other kids so they would like me. My father had died when I was little and I was raised by my mother, who worked hard and tirelessly to instill in me all the proper values in life. I refused to listen and my journey became more and more difficult.

I sat down and cried. I thought being a guardian angel would be sort of fun. My idea of an angel was to fly all over the place and perform miracles. But this was harder than I expected. My coat of feathers felt heavy on my shoulders as I followed Rainbow every step of the way as he began his climb up his magical mountain in search of a dream. He was 10 years old now and the freckles on his face were more prominent than ever, and the kids at school were making fun of him because of how different he looked from the other kids. I hoped he remembered what his mother had told him about how his freckles appeared when the sun kissed him on the cheek.

What was it about this mountain that seemed so familiar? Was it because this was like the mountain I once climbed? The Mountain of Choices, filled with good ones and bad ones, yet I always chose the bad ones because I thought it would be a shortcut to the top. Why am I doing this again? I wished I could just fly up it. It would be so much easier. I tried to take off my coat, but a gust of wind pushed and kept it on my shoulders. God is watching, I thought.

Suddenly in our climb, we came to an abrupt stop. Rainbow's family was selling their house and moving to another neighborhood. For Rainbow, it meant changing schools, leaving old friends behind and making new ones. He had come to a fork in the road, where the path split into two directions.

"I'm confused," I heard Rainbow say to himself.

"That is when the choices you make are tested," I whispered in his ear.

"I'm scared," I could hear him saying. "I don't want to start all over again. I love my house and neighborhood, why do we have to move? I don't know which way to go, right or left?" He looked both ways, then pointed in one direction. "This way seems to have more obstacles, which means I'll need to work hard to make new friends. Or I could go in the other direction and run away from my family just to teach them a big lesson," he said angrily.

"Don't go the *other* way; it is mirrored with deception," I told him, remembering when I once ran away from home because I didn't get my way. I tried waving my arms so he could see me. Rainbow hadn't moved. I wanted to help him make the right decision. "Take time to reflect," I told him, as I stood right in front of him. But his eyes gazed right through me. "If you take the right path, no matter how rocky it looks, you'll be challenged to climb over each rock, but in the end, you'll be rewarded with new and wonderful friendships.

"Remember what I told you, Rainbow. Using your imagination in a positive way will help give you a strong footing. Each crevice on your magical mountain is helping you one step at a time to reach your dream. If you are not careful or move too quickly, you will slip and fall."

I watched as he smiled and started to take the first step in the right direction. He heard me, I thought, or maybe his subconscious remembered the night in the nursery when I warned him of this very situation. I understood Rainbow's anguish—nobody likes change and nobody likes to start all over again. It's like getting used to wearing a comfortable pair of shoes only to have to throw them out and replace them with a new pair that need to be broken in for some time. Rainbow started walking toward a new home and new school.

As he headed in a new direction, Rainbow stumbled and fell. I reached over to help him but the sound of thunder caught my attention. "Ouch!" he cried.

"It's okay to fall," I said to him as I bent down to put my loving arms around him. I wondered if he could feel me hugging him.

"Rainbow, don't forget what I told you the day we sat high up in the tree. Don't worry if you make a mistake; it is through our mistakes that we can learn our greatest lessons. This will be the strength that will help you reach the top of your personal mountain. Keep going forward."

He got up and continued climbing in wonderment up his imaginary mountain, when suddenly he met up with two little white kittens whose eyes were such a deep turquoise that they mesmerized and enchanted him. "Who are you?" he asked joyfully. Rainbow got down on one knee and introduced himself as he cuddled them close to his heart.

"What are your names?"

The first white kitten was biting the other kitten's tail for fun. He turned to Rainbow and said, "My name is Innocent."

"And I'm Dream," said the other kitten as he rubbed up against his legs playfully.

"We are brothers," said Innocent. "We have so much fun playing and running up the mountain to see where it leads."

"We can't wait to see what is around the bend," Dream purred affectionately.

"Today we climbed our first tree," said Innocent, licking his shining coat with pride.

"A small one," Dream hissed at Innocent. "We will conquer a big one, like that one!" he pointed to the tallest tree in the forest with his little furry paw.

Rainbow watched them with his beautiful eyes of blue as they ran around and rolled in the green grass together.

"Look, there's a butterfly! We have to go," said Dream. "We need to see where the butterfly is going."

"Wait! Don't go without me!" Rainbow started to run after them, only to lose them as they disappeared in between the colorful trees and caves that lie in the mountains waiting to be explored.

I kept talking to him as he walked. "This is how we all begin life—full of innocence and dreams, like when you learned how to ride your bicycle and climb a tree."

We walked and I talked and talked, but Rainbow couldn't hear me. He was so full of confidence that he felt he could handle anything that would come his way. He thought he would live forever and nothing could interfere with his journey. But there would be a time when his confidence would be challenged during his climb. Just like a mountain climber, there would be troubling times throughout his journey and he needed to be prepared for the unexpected, but he couldn't see this yet.

As we continued to walk, I felt a weird sensation that overpowered me. I was experiencing a déjà vu moment, as if I had been on this route before.

CHAPTER FIVE

Rainbow's Nightmare

As Rainbow grew older, his personal climb became more challenging and there was nothing I could do to make it easier, except to continue whispering advice in his ear so he could deal with the troubled times. He discovered the terrible moments in school when he was picked on by his peers and fell behind in class. Rainbow felt like he couldn't keep up with the other kids. He wanted to be part of the cool group, even though it was the wrong group to belong to. If things weren't worse enough, Rainbow was feeling uncomfortable with his own body as he was getting closer to puberty.

There wasn't a day that went by that Rainbow didn't cry when he got home. His freckles were the size of pennies, or so he thought, and they were starting to climb up his arms. He towered over everyone in the class and his legs were so long that he had difficulty fitting in his own desk at school. He was losing his confidence and started to become very shy. But, he was grateful to have his best friend, Alder, by his side, who often told him not to worry and reminded him that he could run faster with the basketball and score more points than anyone else on the basketball team. After a hard day at school, the two friends would lock themselves in the bathroom and play with Rainbow's dad's shaving cream and shaver, slathering cream all over themselves to see who got the closest, smoothest shave.

I would wrap my wings around him to bring him comfort and then he'd slowly stop to take a deep breath to say a prayer. He prayed for everyone in school to like him. Rainbow did his best to focus on the good times too. He enjoyed playing basketball, hanging out with a few supportive friends, playing football with his dad and building a table for his mom to surprise her for her birthday.

I asked my higher power for answers to Rainbow's problems. "Why God, are there some children who struggle to be accepted and are bullied for no reason? Why are some of those moms or dads trying to make ends meet while other children never have to worry about food in their belly?" The thunder rolled by and rain began to fall. I knew that this was God's way of saying we are never alone. I caught a glimpse of my past and saw myself as an adult, having the same problems, remembering how scared and uncomfortable I had been in my own skin.

As Rainbow lay in a deep sleep, I covered him with my coat of feathers and hugged him throughout the night. I continued whispering to him: "When we have these unfortunate experiences we become angry; we feel hatred for the first time. We feel shortchanged, lied to, and don't trust anyone.

"That's when we start filling up our invisible knapsack with black rocks of anger, hatred, insecurity and fear. Unfortunately, the load of rocks in your invisible knapsack becomes very heavy and more difficult to carry."

I could see that Rainbow was dreaming, and I found a way to penetrate into his dreams and pass along my wisdom with little golden stars that I'd sprinkle on his chest to melt inside his heart. "When you have a heavy knapsack on your back and you lose your footing on the climb, you may find it difficult to make decisions. Dream, Rainbow, and imagine everything is going smoothly, as you climb a winding path around the mountain. Deep inside this part of the magical mountain is a field that is so wide and tall that you can't see where the other side of the mountain is. The field, with its golden grass and sweet smell, feels like silk rubbing against your skin. You are happy and filled with dreams as you roll on the grass, laughing and having fun. Then suddenly you start to notice the field slowly disappearing as the grass becomes shorter. And, now you're standing in the path of dark clouds that are getting ready to roll in with the oncoming storm.

"This is the unexpected! For example, it's like finding yourself in a situation where your girlfriend suddenly dumps you, you get laid off from your part-time job, or a pet or loved one dies, or like superstar athletes who have setbacks early in their careers."

I was getting through to Rainbow. That night, he dreamt that dark clouds chased him down his mountain. Once he was at the bottom of the mountain, he realized he had no choice but to face up to the unexpected. I whispered, "This is called facing up to responsibility. You have to go through the fog of clouds so you can get back up to climbing your mountain. The more you keep walking, the darker and darker the journey becomes. Like a grouping of umbrellas, the black clouds above cast a shadow over your head. You can't see the blue sky or the sun's rays. You can't even hear a bird chirping. You slip and fall on the wet ground."

I could hear Rainbow talking in his sleep, "Why is this happening to me? Why is the mountain I'm climbing so dark?"

I tried to help him with the answer and whispered: "Rainbow, in the middle of these clouds stop and pray, or meditate. Go within you and find the calmness you need. You will experience stillness that will lead you to the answer you are searching for. Be like a butterfly that flies toward the light, rather than the moth that is comfortable living in the dark. If you stay focused like the mountaineer, you will find your way out of your personal Land of Dark Clouds. If you have faith and trust in yourself, the nightmare you're experiencing will end soon."

I told Rainbow he MUST make a choice. "You can either use your imagination in a positive way and take a deep breath and imagine what your breath looks like. Imagine it to be like white fluffy pillows, butterflies, feathers or hearts reaching out to the blue sky. Stay still; do not rush to make a decision. With all your endurance, strength and trust in yourself, face up to your fear. Or you can choose to not pray or meditate for help, after all what can God do? You may believe that there is no such thing as God, because if there were, he wouldn't let you suffer this way. If he really loved you, he wouldn't let this happen to you in the first place, right? You may feel that you have every right to feel hatred and anger. It makes you feel really good to get revenge. You can use your imagination to create evil to bring the bitterness you're feeling inside to life. This is the path that looks easier because it is called a shortcut.

"What are you going to choose, Rainbow, to get you out of the Land of Dark Clouds?" I tried to carry on a dialogue with Rainbow to help him make the right choice. "Remember the pots and pans in the kitchen that we played with? Remember how your heart felt as we made a bang, then a clang, and a thump? If you feel the same energy as your heart beats fast and furious, remember that it's me trying to get your attention. And I can help you make the right choice. Rainbow, if you make the choice to live in the Land of Dark Clouds, it will be full of negativity, which will weigh you down. You will become the moth who lives in darkness."

I continued on, to the point of exhaustion, so he could hear me and know that I was there for him. "Taking a shortcut to resolve an issue isn't the right answer. You can't run from your problems; you must embrace them. It's one of the reasons why some countries are fighting wars. Leaders of such countries are angry and want revenge for the actions of the past, but instead of being patient and talking through issues, they fill their invisible knapsacks with so much hate that they become too heavy and can't move forward toward peace.

"This is a similar situation many kids like you have in school, like when they don't get along with another classmate. The arguing, fighting, or silent tension can leave you frozen in fear. But the bitterness you carry is like holding your breath, until you can't breathe anymore and you blow up into tiny pieces. You become your own terrorist.

"Whatever choice you make will affect you for the rest of your life. Choose the positive route," I cried loudly through his nightmare. "With a positive attitude, you'll get out of the Land of Dark Clouds."

In his nightmare, Rainbow got down on his knees and wept from the deepest part of his soul. He prayed for the courage to make the right choice. The furious thumping of his heart had slowly quieted, just like when his mother brought him his teddy bear. He lay there with his arms wrapped around himself as the stars from the night sky covered him like a blanket. When he would awaken, he would make the right decision—the decision to face the fear within himself, go to school and stand tall and laugh at himself and his height and freckles. When he did that, everyone wouldn't laugh at him but rather with him. And his confidence in himself would soar.

CHAPTER SIX

Rainbow Looks For Courage

When Rainbow woke up the next morning, I watched him get dressed and begin a new day. With his invisible knapsack, he ventured out the door and continued his rough mountain journey to middle school. "Love is another tool you will need to carry inside your invisible knapsack," I said, although I didn't think he could hear me. "You can't love anyone else unless you love yourself first," a lesson that took me so long to learn when I was human. I couldn't love myself no matter how hard I tried. I was ashamed of what I was becoming—a thief. Stealing chocolate bars was now turning into stealing watches and wallets from people.

After school, Rainbow walked to the edge of a wooded area where there was a river that twisted and turned as it wrapped its way to the top of the mountain. He threw rocks as far as he could to see if they could reach the other side of the river. I watched him, worried that he might slip and fall. As I walked with him, I could feel the ache that sat in his heart. His best friend now had a girlfriend and spent all of his free time with her. It was the same for all the other kids at school. They didn't have time to hang out with him since they had girlfriends or they hung out with other friends. I know he couldn't feel my presence and I started to cry so hard that I watered the flowers below him.

"Sit with me, Rainbow, and don't be afraid of the feeling that is hurting you. Get to know it, talk to it and try and deal with it. Share those feelings with someone you trust, like me." But he was stone-faced and wasn't absorbing anything I was saying. "Talk to your parents, doctor or a teacher," I demanded. "Getting in touch with your feelings is better than burying them deep inside of you." I was angry now that I couldn't help him. "When you bury your fears, or do something you will regret, it'll only make the pain bigger.

"You need to live through the pain and regrets that come your way. When you lose a boyfriend or girlfriend it just means it wasn't meant to be. Having this heartbreak is just as important as the rewards and triumphs. Forget what others think of you, remain positive and persevere on your path of hard work and challenges. Make this journey fun and full of laughter by embracing and learning from it."

I tried so hard to get his attention by climbing a tree and moving its branch so it would fall to the ground in front of him and he would look up and remember when we used to sit in a tree together. But he didn't notice it and walked away. "When you face your fears like the mountain climber, you will have the aspiration to rise to great heights." I yelled while following close behind. I was screaming so loud, the birds could hear me, but why not him? He refused to listen and picked up some speed as if he was running away from me.

Then I heard him say to himself, "I just want to be like everybody else. Why can't I be part of the gang."

I was angry that he didn't see his special gifts. He had the wonderful gift of imagination when he used it in a good way. He was kind. He ran faster and caught more footballs during practice than anyone else on the school team and I knew he would make some great touchdowns one day. I couldn't understand why he didn't realize how precious he really was and, like all his peers, he had a lot to offer.

"Everyone, no matter who we are, all have some unique qualities that make us special," I told him, hoping he was not searching for some answers outside himself. "That is why no two snowflakes are alike."

ᏯᎳᎳᎤ

Years had passed and Rainbow was now a teenager, entering a new phase in his life. He was tall and lanky, his blond hair was losing its natural wave and he now slicked the curl in front of his forehead back so no one would notice it. Unfortunately during this time, he had put some distance between us. He never stopped to pray anymore or listen to my advice, but rather he just kept going on without a care in the world and made careless choices. He wasn't interested in doing his homework, hung around with the wrong crowd and refused to listen to his mother's advice when she tried to help.

One day during his climb up the mountain, Rainbow and I came across monkeys jumping joyfully from tree to tree.

"Come on up!" one monkey motioned to Rainbow.

"What are you doing up there?" said Rainbow.

"We clean up the banana peels that fall on the pathway below so people don't slip on them. We may be monkeys but that doesn't mean that we don't have respect for others."

"I read," said one monkey who was wearing glasses. "I read books on nature and how to take care of the environment. That's why we prefer to live in trees, because trees produce the oxygen to clean the air."

"We have a wonderful life up here," said the monkey with his tail hanging down for Rainbow to grab onto and climb up on.

One monkey was shaking the top of the tree and laughing while another took a coconut and played catch with another little monkey. "Come up, we have so much fun being happy. We're happy because we work hard as a team and we play harder as a family," said an older monkey, who looked like a grandpa because of his furry white goatee.

Then suddenly, as Rainbow was about to reach out for a tail and climb up, he saw a pack of coyotes that seemed to be up to no good. They were smoking and one of them was drinking from a bottle of vodka. Rainbow was curious.

"Where are you going?" asked the monkeys who were jumping up and down.

Rainbow ignored them. He wanted to be a part of something that would fill that empty void inside him, and so he introduced himself to the coyotes and made friends with this gang.

"Rainbow, keep walking. Don't stop and talk to them," I whispered. Suddenly, Rainbow heard the sound of swishing in the distance and he moved toward a clearing where a wide branch in the shape of a palm hung in front of him. He reached up to move it away and see what was making the swishing sound. As he quietly poked his head through the opening he made, he saw a frog sitting on a lily pad with a paintbrush and palette. Swoosh, swoosh, the paintbrush went as he made wide strokes with it.

"I know you're there," said the frog in a deep operatic voice.

"What are you doing?" Rainbow asked.

"What does it look like I'm doing? I'm painting a picture of the sunset," replied the frog without taking his eyes off his canvas.

"Painting a sunset?"

"Don't you have a hobby?" the frog sang in his baritone voice.

"No," said Rainbow, shrugging his shoulders and smirking. "Hobbies are for geeks, anyways."

"Oh really. Well, when you don't have a hobby or something productive to keep you busy, you can get yourself into trouble," the frog replied as he made a long stroke of red.

"You see, I work all day long to help humans by cleaning this pond from all of the serious insect pests. I work very hard for all the scientists in the world who are concerned about what is happening to us frogs, because the health of frogs is closely linked to the health of the environment. Frogs are sensitive to pollution. So my job is to work and work all day long, cleaning everything around me on land and water. I exercise a lot too. I leap from lily pad to lily pad to keep myself in shape. Exercising is good for the heart and having a hobby is also good for the heart."

"Yeah, whatever?" Rainbow said.

"When you have a hobby, your heart is happy and content. I'm passionate about my painting because it gives me a wonderful sense of accomplishment and makes me feel proud to paint colors other than green in the world. And when I'm drained from all my hard work, painting gives me an outlet, and to think this all comes from my heart."

Then Rainbow heard growling in the distance and he turned away from the frog to explore more of his surroundings. There he was back drawn again to the coyotes, as the monkeys jumped from tree to tree and the frog continued to paint. He decided to join the coyotes to get to know them better. Rainbow didn't stop to think of the consequences before he decided to sit with them and listen to everything they had to say.

"How would you like to join our pack?" said the leader of the coyotes. "We have so much fun; we don't have any rules. We do as we please and we don't care about anything but ourselves," he snarled.

Rainbow was intrigued, "Sure," he responded.

In his efforts to belong, I worried that Rainbow didn't see the dangers of following this crowd.

"What have you got in there?" Rainbow pointed to the drunk coyote with the bottle.

"Why don't you figure it out on your own," the coyote tempted Rainbow, handing him the bottle.

I sensed that Rainbow was about to fall victim to the temptations around him. "Following the crowd is okay, Rainbow, but only if it's the right crowd," I reminded him, hoping he would suddenly tap into my words. "Following the wrong crowd can lead to temptation, which can lead to addiction." I wasn't going to give up until I caught his attention. I took off my feathered coat and tried to push the pack away, but they only laughed when one of them lost their balance.

"Rainbow, I've been there," I said. "Don't listen to them, they are not your friends. They're evil animals who have come to tempt you and lead you in the wrong direction. It's a trick, a bad trick! Go play with the monkeys, they will show you good clean fun."

Rainbow looked to the right at the beautiful flowers where I was standing. He was listening, I thought. "Despite their joyful appearance, like these gorgeous flowers, these 'fun friends' can be poisonous, making you very sick. Giving into temptation weakens your endurance to complete your journey of life. Can you imagine if a mountain climber kept eating junk food every day? His health would get worse and, over time, it would destroy his stamina.

"If you choose this direction, you'll suddenly find yourself sliding very quickly down the mountain; twisting and turning as if a mudslide was carrying you away. Eventually, you'll be thrown off a cliff and... SPLAT! You'll hit the bottom of the mountain. That's when you must reach inside yourself and find the strength you need to start climbing up again."

"Come with us," beckoned the gang of coyotes, "We're not going to hurt you. We'll protect you." I was furious. How dare they. But I wasn't the only one desperate to save a boy from the pitfalls of evil—I could see an angel accompany each of the coyotes. The angels were also crying as they looked on helplessly.

Still, I wasn't ready to give up on Rainbow. I had to try one more time to reach him. "Rainbow, I'm worried you've forgotten everything I taught you when you could see and hear me. Remember, when you get confused, stop, sit still and listen; listen and you will hear my voice. Some people who call themselves friends will tempt you into the world of addiction. It isn't just alcohol or drugs. There are all kinds of addictions: money, shopping, gambling, work, food, smoking, sex, computer games, the Internet and cyber sex. And you have the power to say NO. Do you hear me?"

Rainbow turned and walked away. I felt like I had failed Rainbow. I was now following the other angels who followed the coyotes as they walked with my Rainbow. How could Rainbow, who made me laugh on so many days, reach this point? I was puzzled and I needed direction.

"Why do you let this happen God?" I took my fist and raised it toward the sky.

Lightening shot across the sky, then hard rain started to fall. I knew then that God was counting on me to be the teacher to guide Rainbow in the right direction.

"But how can I, if he can't hear me?"

Thunder crashed and shook the trees. I could see the beady eyes of the coyotes, now looking straight at me like small pinpoints in the dark. The coyotes now led Rainbow into a hidden clearing that was surrounded by prickly vines. The vines twisted around the trees circling the clearing and were topped with dark leaves that took the shape of ugly heads beckoning the coyotes to move further along the mysterious path.

I followed them as they came upon glistening icicles, and high above them on a ledge sat a beautiful woman wearing a long coat in rainbow colors. Her wings changed from silver to gold as she welcomed the pack of coyotes with Rainbow. Her fingernails were made of delicate pink roses; her eyelashes glistened like freshly fallen snowflakes; her teeth shone like natural pearls; her skin looked like soft pink suede and her eyes were as blue-green as the calmest ocean. The coyotes and Rainbow got down on their knees to bow to her with admiration.

"You are the most beautiful woman I have ever seen," I heard Rainbow say.

"Rainbow, it's a trick, an illusion," I yelled. "Don't be fooled. She's not good, she's an evil creature. She *represents* addiction!"

"I love you, Rainbow, and I will dedicate myself to helping you when you get lonely, sad, or depressed," she purred. "I will be there during your weakest moments to give you a gift of strength to get you through the most difficult times in your life," she seductively moved around in all her splendor.

"I'm assigned to Rainbow!" I yelled at her, but she quickly took her long strong arm and pushed me aside.

"Rainbow, you must listen to me!" my wings flapped in desperation. "If you follow her down this path, it will only be a temporary escape to her never-never land, a place that doesn't really exist except within your mind. If you get trapped here, you'll feel like a hamster spinning around and around inside of it and going nowhere. It's a place where nobody grows up."

"I want to be with you forever," she whispered to him.

"No, Rainbow, listen to me. I'm your supporter, your guide forever," I pleaded.

"You make me happy," Rainbow said to her, reaching out to be loved.

"I love you, Rainbow! Remember the first word you learned… love. Your parents, friends and I love you. You don't need her," I wept.

The evil creature gathered up her young followers and lead them through dark pathways until they came to an opening in a cave at the edge of the murky stream. She gracefully sat under the trees that lined the entrance of her domain and I instantly understood why they called the trees weeping willows. They cry for every lost soul that was captured by this creature of emptiness. I watched her as she seductively handed a package to Rainbow and the other coyotes.

"Rainbow, go quickly into your invisible knapsack and pull out your tool of ENDURANCE and say... NO!"

My voice was carried away by the wind.

CHAPTER SEVEN

Autumn's Tormented Climb

*F*or the first time, all the memories of my former life were starting to make sense. I bent over the edge of the river to see my reflection. Yes, it really was me.

I had met the creature of addiction during my lifetime. The river showed me a picture of myself as a young teenager caught up with a pack of coyotes who were living life in the fast lane. I accepted the seductive invitation of taking drugs and drinking, filling me up with emptiness. I found myself taking the first step on the path of destruction and meeting the same creature called Addiction that Rainbow had become entranced with in the clearing.

It began so innocently as I went out with a bunch of kids to a party. I remember I was too shy to dance with one boy I thought was cute. My body was frozen; my tongue was tied. Then one of my friends offered me something to 'help'—they brought along a case of beer, some vodka and marijuana, and assured me that the stuff would loosen me up. I took several puffs on the joint and drank the vodka, and soon I felt like I had hit a home run. I no longer felt any inhibitions and the tension began to melt away. I felt wonderful!

But I couldn't stop drinking, and soon I needed more alcohol to go along with my drugs. The beer flowed down my throat, giving me a wonderful sensation like a refreshing waterfall that soothed an overheated body. I felt like I had won the World Series.

I don't remember what happened next. The years that followed were a big blur. I just know that when I finally looked in the mirror, I didn't look so wonderful. Staring back at me was some sort of monster. I lost my good looks, my innocence and myself. My bones were poking out of my body as if they were knives.

I could remember few other details of my life on Earth with my angel, Summer, guiding me. All I know is that for some reason God saw something in me that I couldn't see, enough to think that I had earned his forgiveness and had enough faith in me to be Rainbow's angel. God was a mystery to me—I didn't know what his plan was or why I was assigned to this very precious child. All I knew, looking back to when I met Rainbow, was that I was slowly learning that with hard work and discipline and trust in myself I could make the right choices.

The rest of the day, I watched helplessly while Rainbow drank alcohol and took drugs. His soft facial features were disappearing before me as he was transforming into a coyote. His eyes were piercing through the dark like a wild animal. I had no choice but to follow him. After all, underneath that skin and bones was Rainbow, trapped in the world of addiction. He made his choice and his troublesome journey took us aboard a white-water rafting trip that he accepted from the creature Addiction.

Although I knew it was futile, I yelled: "There are no shortcuts up this magical mountain!" He refused to listen. The drugs and alcohol numbed the pain in his heart and dampened the sound of me pounding on it like the pots and pans. We twisted and turned around the imaginary river, which led to nowhere. The waves were overpowering but he kept surging, loving every minute of the high he was experiencing. He felt he could do anything!

"I'm Superman," he hollered as he flew through the air. "What a great feeling! I'm untouchable!" I had never heard such confidence in Rainbow.

Then we heard a BANG! The trip came to an abrupt halt. Rainbow was thrown ashore and abandoned, and lonelier than ever before. He was back where he began, at the bottom of his mountain. Only this time, his feelings of anxiety had deepened within him and he felt even emptier inside. He drank more and started to fly again and again. It was a never-ending ride to nowhere. Months went by and I was exhausted from all my yelling. I pounded and banged his heart. The more I did, the more he took drugs to numb any feelings that he once had for me or emotions he felt during his life.

He sat in a corner, feeling ashamed for what he had done to himself. But the only way he felt he could deal with his shame was to keep drinking and doing drugs. Loved ones tried to help—his parents cried, I cried, but Rainbow was no longer our Rainbow. He was a mean vicious coyote living with a pack of animals controlled by addiction.

I watched him as he lay there shamefully looking out onto the horizon contemplating what had just happened to him. There was silence, a wonderful silence and all I hoped for was that he would stop long enough to meditate or pray and ask for my guidance. He walked over to the river of despair with his head hung low. Looking into the river, he saw his reflection and was horrified to see what he had become.

I could feel the sense of hopelessness overcome him. "Why did I do this?" I could hear Rainbow whimper to himself. "I wasted so much time and the best months of my life." He was speaking to me straight from his heart. Finally, I had his attention.

"There are consequences for each choice we make," I said to him.

"I loved the way I felt when I was having my fun, but then everything wasn't fun anymore," he responded. "It all became a terrible ride that I just couldn't stop or get off."

"You can't keep this up," I said. "Taking drugs and getting drunk will only get you into serious trouble, like hurting yourself or getting arrested and going to jail. Sure, you'll feel like you've climbed the highest mountain, but it doesn't last. As quickly as you've gone up it, you'll come crashing down and experience feelings of guilt, shame and low self-esteem. If only you didn't follow the crowd of coyotes and instead checked in with me, you would have seen that I would never have steered you in the wrong direction or given you the wrong advice. Rainbow, from here on, you must keep feeding yourself with wonderful words of love, surround yourself with those who care about you, and then you'll be able to trust yourself to make the right decision."

"I don't think I can. Nobody likes me and I can't succeed at anything. I'm so confused," he said sadly.

"Keep still, pray, know that I am with you. We don't have to get up and rush. Just take your time and assess your situation." I wiped the tears from his foggy blue eyes.

"Later in life, Rainbow, when you approach a similar situation where you're feeling uncomfortable, you must deal with the problem head-on and remember that drugs and alcohol don't solve it. They're merely a temporary solution. Instead of coming to terms with your shyness, you relied on the alcohol and drugs to cover up what you were feeling inside.

"But as you've seen with the deceitful creature, addiction wears many faces and disguises. She is the greatest magician the world has ever known," I said, taking the opportunity to reinforce the evils of addiction. "Her coat was the color of a rainbow but it turned into a heavy black coat made of tar once addiction wrapped her arms around you. Her wings went from gold to charcoal and her fingernails transformed from roses to thorns. Her pearly teeth grew into fangs while her eyelashes made of snowflakes become snarling snakes. Her turquoise eyes resembling a calm ocean became the violent tsunami that hungers for your life.

"This is what addiction really looks like, Rainbow. She creates an illusion that brings you into her life, only to leave you in a tangled web of false promises and broken dreams."

Just as I thought I was making some progress in getting Rainbow to turn his back on addiction, the evil creature reappeared. This time she looked even more beautiful, disguised as a glowing angel all dressed in white. She could see me, but refused to acknowledge my presence and my relationship with Rainbow as his protector. I told Rainbow that I knew from experience that once you've tasted addiction it hides in the darkest corner and waits for the perfect time to reappear so that it has more opportunity with your soul to make it her own.

"Trust me, I'm the one who loves you the most," she said softly. "If you come with me, I will fly you to the top of the highest mountain even faster than you can climb it."

Her pitch was enticing and I was afraid Rainbow couldn't turn his back. "This trip will be the journey of a lifetime—up through the magenta sky and all the way to the Big Dipper and back. Your confidence will soar; there will be no stopping you. I invite you to experience this incredible spectacle of fireworks in the sky."

I tried hopelessly to reason with Rainbow. "Don't destroy your life and your dreams by going with her," I said. "If you accept her invitation, your descent will be even harder, and it will be tougher to climb back up again."

Rainbow wasn't listening to me anymore. I continued to speak to him in case there was a slight chance he would sit down and find the courage inside himself to say NO!

"Remember," I urged, "what goes up the mountain must come down." I remembered these same words when I was Rainbow's age and now they were coming back to haunt me. My own guardian angel, Summer, tried to keep me off the course of destruction with the same plea.

"Each time you give in to temptation," Summer once told me, "you will short-circuit your dream with addiction at your side. You have avoided how to deal with your problems and your invisible knapsack is bursting at the seams from all the heavy rocks you are carrying."

"Forgive me, Summer, wherever you are," I said up to the sky, wondering if angels have angels to look after them. "How did I find my way back?"

As a young woman, I kept going round and round in circles like a cat after its own tail—only to bite itself on the behind over and over again. I abused and wasted my life away. I lost interest in everything but the drug. I fell into a dark and lonely place. Nothing went right for me; the people I met were not my friends, but addicts who had problems too. There was a violent war churning inside me like land mines exploding in fields that were once play-grounds. I came to believe that the only thing that could stop the explosion lay at the bottom of a bottle or at the butt of a drug. Every invitation I received was an invitation to hell, yet I accepted it. It wasn't until late in life that I finally surrendered myself to God and assumed responsibility for my addiction, my personal disease. Even though I fought the war inside me, I felt so ashamed for the time I wasted and wished I had just made the right choices earlier on.

Hitting rock bottom taught me my hardest lesson—that once you are lost on the wrong path nobody can help you, not even your parents, friends or doctors. Only you can make the commitment to getting well and staying well.

I stood by and watched Rainbow suffer and wished that I could wave a magic wand and change everything back to the way it was. Then I remembered what God had instructed me to do; that I was NOT to control the outcome of Rainbow's journey. I had to accept that it was his choice and the dream that he kept in his locket was between him and God.

"This is your journey Rainbow," I said calmly. "You have a choice to make. Is this the life you want to live—empty, meaningless and alone? Or, do you want to find your way back?"

CHAPTER EIGHT

Rainbow Makes a Choice

"I never said climbing a mountain was easy. If I go back to that night in the nursery when we first met, I told you that you must make a commitment to your personal climb," I told Rainbow, who finally accepted my help. "Yes, there will be times when you'll slip and rocks will fall below your feet. But it's no different than when your teacher tells you to repeat doing your homework. These are challenges that will help you to grow, if you embrace them."

Rainbow sat still and spoke quietly. "Help me. I can't live this life anymore and I want help. I want to be the Rainbow I know I can be."

Rainbow was now sitting by a tall pine tree with branches that moved gracefully in the breeze. "I'm so confused. Help me find my way," Rainbow kept saying over and over again, holding his hands so they wouldn't shake uncontrollably.

"But what choice do I make?" Rainbow asked in prayer to me. The anguish he was feeling was making him feel sick with worry about his future. "Do I surrender myself completely and know that I'm powerless over my addiction? Or do I use my imagination in a positive way and know that I have my guardian angel beside me who will give me the strength to overcome my addiction? Or do I look inside my invisible knapsack and pull out the tool called endurance and get the strength I need through the power of prayer and find my way to treatment?

"YES, YES, YES, I should do all of them!" Rainbow assured himself.

I was overjoyed to hear those beautiful words of submission come from Rainbow's mouth. He was now in his late teens and there would be more opportunities that would lie ahead for him to turn around and make a new life for himself. He just had to be very careful he didn't lose the early years of his precious life. I watched him embrace his future, starting all over again. He was far from the beautiful boy I once knew. He was thin and bony. His cheeks were sunken, and his blond hair had changed to a muddy brown. He walked with his head down full of shame and silence. He missed so much of school—the lessons, the homework and exams—that he didn't earn any credits and needed to make up his year.

I knew he was searching within himself to get some spiritual help for his journey. He stopped to think of his past year and his destructive life. Everyone from his teachers to his friends no longer understood why he chose the direction he went. His parents and some of his old friends from school tried to give him encouragement and show him his options. "We are here for you, to support you in your recovery. We love you, Rainbow," said his old friend. "We need you back on the team." Addiction broke his family's heart. But Rainbow couldn't reach out for help until now.

He started to pray: "I'll embrace my recovery with a positive and exciting approach to a new life, even though I'm very scared to take this step."

While Rainbow prayed, I took him by the hand and told him to speak from his heart. "Use your imagination in a positive way and visualize a treatment center that looks like a castle sitting up high on a white cloud above the mountain you are climbing." I wrapped my arms around him tightly as he entered the treatment facility he had chosen after consulting with his family. I could feel how scared he was as we approached the front entrance of the facility. Visualizing it as a castle, he bravely knocked on the door and a majestic wizard appeared.

"Hi, my name is Rainbow and I need your help," he said hesitantly. "I'm an alcoholic and a drug addict and I'm seeking treatment. I lost all the things I love, like my dream, being truly happy and healthy, and my supportive family. Are you the wizard that will show me the way back?"

The wizard nodded, took Rainbow by the hand and said: "I will show you the tools you will need in order to succeed in your recovery. You see, Rainbow, I know what you are going through better than you think. I was once like you—lost, confused, lonely, and convinced that only drugs and alcohol could drown out the feelings of hopelessness I felt inside. It wasn't until I made the choice to come to the castle in the sky and meet a wizard who would show me the way out of my dark hole that I got the help I needed. My wizard had also been an addict. Through determination, self-reflection, therapy and years and years of knowledge and reaching out to others, he became a powerful influence for others. He was living proof that there is hope for all us addicts. There are so many wonderful examples of this, including celebrities, politicians, musicians, athletes and everyday people who struggle on the road to recovery."

We followed the wizard down a long corridor, his gown flowing. Along the corridor, Rainbow and I could see paintings hung on the walls with images of Rainbow's life. He saw in one painting how happy he looked before he made the wrong choice and took the wrong path. Another painting showed him squeezing into his desk at school, feeling awkward about his height and freckles. Still another captured the dark day he spent with the coyotes. As he walked along the corridor, the paintings got darker and darker showing him how sad and depressing his life had become. One of the darkest paintings showed the deep sadness and hurt his family was feeling as they tried to desperately save him. Rainbow was reminded by the wizard to stop and examine each of them, and take a moral inventory of himself. "With me by your side, admit to all the wrongs you have made and all the people you have harmed, and then start a new life all over again with a positive attitude," said the wizard. "Only you can empower yourself to change your paintings of sad images from your past to more happy and healthier images of who you want to be."

The wizard then took Rainbow into a large room with a big table in the center. Seated around it were the same coyotes Rainbow encountered on his addiction journey. One of the coyotes with dark sunken eyes stood in the corner of the room. He kept repeating over and over again, "I can't do this. Two of the planets I was born under are Neptune and Mars. They conflict with each other and they pull me down."

Rainbow watched as the coyote, whose bones were poking through his body, showed the other coyotes in treatment with him, a thick, heavy book with pictures of planets. "See look, it reads: 'Neptune leads to self-deception, while Mars is the planet of destruction, subject to impulsive or violent tendencies.' On top of this, I was born in the Chinese New Year of the rat. So no matter how hard I try, I can't do this. My parents forced me to come here, but I really don't want to be here because there's no use."

The wizard put his arm around Rainbow and said, "Nobody can force anyone into treatment, although having support is essential through your recovery. Ultimately, it has to be your choice! The coyote is not the way he is because of the planets—it is because he chooses to dwell on the negative aspects of life and, therefore, he chooses not to take responsibility for his disease. Being in denial is just one more obstacle to recovery. The coyote doesn't realize that many other wonderful people have been born under those same planets and it didn't pull them down. It is what you make out of your life and circumstances that really counts. Rainbow, God gives us a gift of life. What we do with our life is our gift back to him and ourselves.

"For example, the year of the rat can be looked at in two ways—negative or positive," continued the wizard. "The positive side is that the rat is very intelligent, capable of many wonderful things, and is not necessarily the 'dirty' rat many see him as. So you see, Rainbow, it all comes down to attitude and a strong commitment to getting well."

Then the wizard turned his attention to all the patients at the table. He opened up a treasure box on the table and pulled out a recipe card with ingredients to make a cake. "This card tells you how to make your cake of sobriety. Start by taking your tears and admitting to yourself that you are completely powerless over your addiction and surrender your addiction, your disease, into a bowl. Add the shame you feel for the harm you have done to people and admit to yourself that you are willing to make amends. Admit your mistakes and go within yourself and pray for guidance and help. These secret ingredients all come from inside of you. If you have trust in yourself, and faith in me, you will create a decadent cake that oozes with the sweetness of a new life," said the wizard. "When you bite into it, you will savor the flavor of each ingredient and change the way you live. This cake will awaken the new you. Think of it as a kind of rebirth, or birthday."

As part of Rainbow's recovery, he was required every morning to get up at the crack of dawn and do his chores before even having breakfast. Cleaning the toilets, washing the floor and making his bed. There was no socializing with anyone else in the treatment center.

Rehab was difficult. Twice a day, there was group therapy, where you would 'spill out your guts' to others and express how difficult it was to climb out of a dark hole and embrace a new life. But Rainbow had accepted the challenge and he was turning his life around. He was learning so many tools he needed to continue his life journey, such as learning to eat properly, exercising and keeping a daily journal to express his emotions on paper. Perhaps the hardest part of this process for Rainbow was exposing himself to other people. The center helped him deal with this part of recovery by bringing in inspirational speakers who would speak to the group about their own recovery.

Once Rainbow, the coyotes and other recovering addicts had spent an adequate time in the center, the wizard reminded them of the recipe they should always carry with them in times of trouble. "Your cake will replace the negative rocks that you have been carrying. Your load will now becomes lighter," said the wizard as he helped put the birthday cake that Rainbow finished making inside his knapsack.

Now revitalized, Rainbow thanked the wizard, wished the coyotes well on their continual recovery and said goodbye to all of them. The wizard reminded him that his friends, family and the people who he met at the center were all available to him when he needed them. He was greeted by his family, just outside the castle, to support him on his journey through life.

"I'm a new me," Rainbow announced as he embraced his family. "This is my recovery; you can love me, but you can't help me," he smiled, repeating the words I once told him. "I will look forward to my climb one day at a time, up my personal mountain and know that inside me is my recipe for a successful recovery."

His sobriety or birthday cake was as light as the feathers of a baby eagle and as tall as the mountain he was about to climb again. It displayed layer after layer of knowledge, sweetened from the fruits of labor of his support system. It poked out of his knapsack, like a tower reaching so far up that it touched the wizard's castle high among the clouds. As we walked together up the mountain,

I had to keep moving out of the way to prevent the cake from smacking me in the face.

We walked slowly and quietly while Rainbow reflected out loud. "I hope I can do this, stay clean and work on my addiction one day at a time."

With my hand pressed against his heart I repeated the words that the wizard told him before he left the castle. "Now that you are leaving treatment, you might feel like you can handle life and its obstacles but you must be careful and take your time! Like the mountain climber who slips and falls and must begin all over again, you'll need to be even more prepared for this climb. The mountain climber doesn't get overconfident even though he's familiar with the mountain's terrain. Instead, he takes the same steps carefully, one at a time. And don't assume that you can just start climbing again without any protection. Remember, there is always the unexpected."

I wanted to test him to see how ready he was for this journey. "What do you do when you get confused or tempted to drink or take drugs?"

"You say the serenity prayer," he said. The prayer is an important part of the recipe of the sobriety cake. "God, grant me the serenity to accept the things I cannot change, the courage to change the things I can, and the wisdom to know the difference," Rainbow said humbly.

With my hand still on his heart, I cautioned Rainbow that treatment doesn't mean you have gotten rid of your addiction. "She is always there on your doorstep when you leave for school in the morning or go out with friends, saying, 'I miss you, come out to play with me one more time. I love you. I'm lonely, and I won't hurt you.'"

"I know what to do. I'll just say NO!" yelled Rainbow. "If I don't, my precious cake will melt away and I'll be back living in that dark lonely place called hopelessness.

"I plan to hang out with the right friends, go to meetings, and get a sponsor. I won't jump into making quick decisions."

It was wonderful to finally connect with Rainbow. I had great hope that he would make it through this tough period in his life and eventually make his dreams come true.

CHAPTER NINE

Trees Up Ahead

Rainbow and I were halfway up his magical mountain when he found a new place of discovery and intrigue. He was going to return to school to finish where he had left off to get his credits so he could be accepted into university. Rainbow felt more enlightened and interested as he was back in shape mentally and physically to continue his climb up his mountain.

As he climbed he stopped to admire a winding path lined with tree houses on either side that reached as far up as he could see. One tree house was made out of sticks and crumbled leaves; it barely sat on the top of the tree.

"I wonder who lives inside?" he said to himself.

Rainbow continued walking along the path and came across another tree house, this time made of stones. It sat halfway up the tree trunk.

"I wonder who lives inside this tree house?" he said as he looked up.

A few more steps along, Rainbow discovered another tree house made of precious gems—emeralds, diamonds, rubies and sapphires. This house wasn't sitting up high on its tree but instead it sat in front of a garden made of mirrors. In all its glory, the tree house made of gems created rainbows in the puddles of water along the path.

I could see that Rainbow wondered who lived inside this one too. We sat quietly by a pond close by and looked up at each of the tree houses. The one made of twigs and crumbled leaves was shaky and barely standing. The one made of stones was stronger, but some of the pebbles and rocks were slowly chipping away. The last one, an elaborate house, blinded you like the sun's rays hitting your eyes.

As Rainbow looked at each of them, he wondered again about the people who lived inside them. I could almost hear his thoughts. Which one believes in themselves the most? Which one is working toward his dream, keeping the golden locket shiny and near his heart? Which one is rich in spirit and knows the direction of his dream as he dedicates his life to it? Which one has no fear to go after his dreams? Which one is confused and does not have the confidence to reach for the impossible dream? And which one has wasted his dream?

Rainbow approached each of the tree houses to meet the people who lived inside. He first approached the tree house made of sticks and leaves. I pressed my hand on his heart and spoke to him through his heart. "Be careful," I warned him just before he climbed up high and out of sight. "You don't want to shake the tree and have the house come tumbling down. Move smoothly and quietly. Are you there yet?" I watched and listened for an answer.

"I'm here," he spoke with confidence. I told him to knock on the door softly. The door opened and Rainbow stepped inside.

"What do you see?"

"There is a young child sitting with a smile on his face. His eyes are a beautiful deep blue and his hair is thick with curls. He is smiling at me."

"Hi. My name is Rainbow," he told the child, reaching out his hand.

"My name is Hope," said the little boy. His eyelashes glistened in the light.

"How can you live in this house? Are you not afraid your house will fall down?" Rainbow asked.

"Oh no, you see I keep my golden locket shining nice and bright, and close to my heart. I have a dream," said Hope. "That is why I sit so tall up in my house; so I can see where I'm going. I will make my dream come true because I believe that no matter what happens I have the inner strength to stand tall. I'm grateful for everything I receive, good and bad, because this is what I learn from. That's why my house will never fall down."

Rainbow climbed back down the tree and told me he was inspired by what he heard. "He believes in his dream," he told me. "He isn't going to fall into temptation, which would lead him in another direction."

Now Rainbow was even more curious to meet the other people who lived in the other tree houses along the road. "This is a stronger house," he said as he climbed the house made of stones, "but it's a little frightening because every time I take a step, a stone falls below my feet."

At the door, Rainbow used the knocker made of steel. The door opened wide and a woman appeared dressed in gray clothes to match her house of stones. Her hair was long and flowing—the color of the raven that flies high above her house. Her eyes were as deep as the earth.

"Hi, my name is Rainbow."

"My name is Fear."

"Why is your house made of gray stones, sitting halfway up the tree?"

"I'm scared to go up any further," said Fear. "I know I have a dream in my heart. I just don't have the courage to take a look. I'm afraid that I will fail, so I sit here looking at my tarnished locket every day and don't take any chances."

"But you have a dream!" Rainbow encouraged her. "Don't be afraid, you can do it!"

"I can't. The load is too heavy for me to carry," she tells him sadly. "It's too hard for me. I'm tired of climbing up my tree to see which way I should go. I'm stuck. I will be here until the day I die!"

At that point, Rainbow knew there was nothing he could say to change her mind. Like her home, her mind was set in stone.

Rainbow approached the last tree house on his journey. It was by far the most beautiful home. He walked toward its front entrance on ground level, up a path landscaped in diamonds. Along the path was a rose garden made of rubies and trees made of emeralds. There was a bluebird made of sapphires sitting atop a roof made of silver.

He knocked on the gold door and it opened slowly. Sitting on the floor was the smallest man you could ever meet. In fact, you almost needed a magnifying glass to see him. Surrounding him were broken mirrors that showed the very sad reflection of his life. Each mirror represented a dream that once belonged to him and was now broken into tiny pieces.

"My name is Rainbow. What's your name?"

"My name is Waste." His voice sounded like a whimpering puppy.

"Why is your house so beautiful on the outside, but not on the inside. Why are the mirrors shattered and destroyed?"

"I abused my dream," said Waste. "I went down the wrong path. I was lazy. I didn't want to work hard, so I took a shortcut. The more shortcuts I took, the more my dreams kept breaking apart. I keep my locket broken in two, inside this glass box. I cry all the time, as I see what terrible things I have done along the way. I'm so ashamed of myself, ashamed that I wasted my life when I had so much more to offer than anyone else. I was born with many gifts and had a family that had so much to give me.

Now I don't know where my family is or what my dream is. It is gone forever. That is why I live in a house that is beautiful on the outside. It hides what I'm truly feeling on the inside."

"It's not too late to change your life," Rainbow encouraged him.

"I just don't have the confidence inside of me to lift my tree house and carry it to the top to look and see where I'm going," he said. "I'm so loaded down with possessions and material things that I just can't let go of them."

Rainbow reminded him that he could help people by sharing his wealth with others.

"No, I wouldn't do that. I like my possessions. They're all that I have left. Everyone admires my tree house as they walk by. I could never let that go and start all over. I can't leave the inside of my house and go outside to see the house as others see it. I'm locked inside with nothing to offer. I like to be left alone with all my broken dreams and my gold locket inside a glass box."

Discouraged, Rainbow came out of the house and we continued to walk up the mountain. I whispered to him that no matter how hard we try we can't ever convince someone that they can achieve their dreams. It has to come from within the person. "When we waste what we have to offer, like this small man, life becomes a tragedy," I told him. "Rainbow, I know you're wondering why he can't pick up his shattered life and try again. Why he couldn't just use all the tools inside his knapsack to make a better life. Even his guardian angel is beside him working hard to encourage him to pick up the pieces."

I told Rainbow that Waste didn't take the time to look inside. Instead of having faith in himself to make his dreams come true, he had become consumed with his obsession. "Look at how sad Fear's life is. She only gets halfway up the tree and becomes scared because she thinks she is going to fail. She doesn't realize that she needs to learn in order to succeed. She has everything she needs to make her dream come true, but she refuses to use the tools that we have been talking about," I told him.

"But look at the little boy named Hope. Even with all the difficulties he has with his house of twigs and crumbled leaves, he still has faith in himself. He's determined to make his dream come true. He is the young mountaineer who will reach the top of the mountain."

Rainbow paused to reflect on the three people he had met and realized that he was more determined than ever to live a life of hope.

CHAPTER TEN

Rainbow Goes Sailing

*L*ike most mountains, the one that Rainbow continued to climb had several hidden passages within it, just waiting to be discovered, like the valleys and trails that lead climbers to other mountains. Rainbow and I explored his mountain, walking and climbing it until our feet ached. I never thought an angel's feet could be so sore! As we approached one edge of the mountain to take a rest, we looked out to discover the deepest crystal blue ocean in front of us and followed a trail down a grassy hill on the other side of the mountain to its sandy shores. Rainbow had blisters on his feet, too, and we both took the opportunity to soak our feet in the cool water.

"God why can't I fly? What's the purpose of these wings if I can't fly?" I asked. There was no thunder or lightning this time, only the sound of an eagle's cry high above. God's message this time: it was not the time for me to fly.

"Look, in the distance, there's a ship!" Rainbow hollered with excitement. "I need to get on board so I can cross the ocean that separates this mountain and get to the other side."

Again, flashes of my memory returned as the ship got closer to shore. I remembered being on the same ship a long time ago and making a choice on it that I later regretted. I began to weep as I remembered myself as a young girl who bought a ticket in the wrong direction, the direction of loneliness and despair.

There was no other path to get to the other side, so Rainbow had no choice but to board the ship. Once he boarded, it was like being in school again, a place where hard work and discipline were required in order to have a successful voyage. Again, he had to make the choice to apply himself and take responsibility for his choices. I recognized some of the passengers—they were his old schoolmates—and I couldn't help but think about how they came from many walks of life and each one lived by different values.

"What do you mean by values?" asked Rainbow, who had just celebrated his 18th birthday.

I was surprised to hear his question. Did Rainbow hear my thoughts? Or did my emotions create vibrations like a tuning fork hitting him over the head?

I whispered to Rainbow, who was looking up at the seagulls circling above him. "By values, I mean little gifts that you give yourself every day of your life," I said to Rainbow as I watched two seagulls fight over a scrap of food. "They're what you stand for—honesty, hard work, consideration, responsibility and strong family relationships. Everyone has different values, and when you decide what your values are they become your personal mission statement." Rainbow nodded his head with a smile as he put his hand on his heart to hear more.

Suddenly a flock of seagulls swooped down onto the deck as the ship's chef threw out more scraps just outside the kitchen door. As we moved away to avoid the aggressive birds in front of us, I started to shout my words above all the racket so Rainbow didn't become distracted and lose focus.

The birds picked up their food and flew away. "On a professional level, corporations show values through their brand. You see brands everywhere. For example, you may notice a picture on a box of cereal. This picture represents what a company believes in, such as good health and nutrition," I said, lowering my voice now.

"I know I have some values," he said to himself as he sat down on the bench that held the life preservers at the front of the ship.

"Yes, you do!" I shouted for joy, doing a cartwheel in front of Rainbow and hoping he could see me. "You're carrying your values inside your invisible knapsack.

"By visiting the people who live in the tree houses you've learned the values of hard work and never giving up, like the values of the little boy named Hope," I said as I jumped up to try and fly off the guardrails, but ended up landing in the water. "Angel overboard," I yelled. Then a few seagulls swooped down to pick me up with their beaks and carry me safely back on the deck. My feathers were soaked and my halo needed adjusting, but I was still determined to teach Rainbow. "Always remember your value of self-respect and know that it's one day at a time."

"I need to remember that I have to say NO!" Rainbow replied to himself. I knew then that he was listening.

I watched Rainbow as he got up to stretch out his long legs over my feathered coat. "As you go along in life, your values can grow, or they can shrink," I cautioned him. "You can add or subtract to your mission statement, or change it completely. It's always a good idea to write up a mission statement and hang it up on your bedroom wall to remind you of who you are."

"I'm determined to take responsibility to make life better," he said. I felt a sense of relief that Rainbow had everything he needed for this voyage across the ocean. He had his values and the locket with his secret dream in it.

Rainbow was confident but I was still nervous and scared to be on the ship that once drowned my life. It was my wasted voyage and it was filled with horrors. I knew this ship all too well, its secrets and poisons that were hidden within the life preservers, deep inside the cabins and buried with the cargo.

I had nothing to fear because I felt Rainbow's endurance getting stronger by the day. He kept up with his recovery program. He always said his serenity prayer and made sure that he hung out with the right crowd of kids. By doing this, he was taking a bite into the cake he made with the same recipe the wizard gave him. Still, I also knew that Rainbow faced more choices and that his most sacred value—his self-respect—would be vigorously tested on this ship. He was being invited to one of his most popular classmate's party, where everyone who mattered would show up.

"This voyage is up to you, Rainbow," I said as he sat up high on a chair at the front of the boat. "It may go smooth or it could be rough waters ahead," I told him, "Don't forget that negative thoughts like anger and revenge will sink this ship. When you indulge in alcohol or drugs, you're only welcoming back negative and life-threatening emotions that will leave you swimming with the sharks.

"Remember the important tools that you carry in your invisible knapsack—they will become your life jacket of support." I recall hearing these same words of wisdom from my angel, Summer, many years ago.

I wasn't sure if he was listening to me as he walked around the deck, looking out to the ocean. "You'll encounter the same trials and tribulations that you experienced as you first climbed the mountain," I said. "The waves will grow taller, pounding against the ship. The rain will come down hard, blinding you. You will get seasick as you toss and turn in the storm you created inside yourself when you made the wrong choice. But if you're full of love and peace, show your joy for life, and have faith in yourself, then all these wonderful emotions become your life jacket of support."

"May I have your attention, please?!" All eyes looked toward the center of the deck where a creature, disguised as an elegant man, stood, one that I knew all too well.

It was the steward. He hadn't aged a bit since I saw him years ago. He seemed very confident and graceful, draped in a beautiful royal blue coat with gold epaulettes. His coat covered much of his body, including the tail he dragged behind him along the floor. He still wore a monocle on one eye. With all the majesty of a royal messenger at a ball, he held up a scroll and began to read a special announcement to all the passengers.

"Don't read it," I said to myself. "Change the wording! Please, God, have him change the wording." But it was too late.

"In order to be accepted to the first-class section of the ship with the majority of the passengers, you need to be cool," read the steward. "In order to be cool, accept our invitation to a party with a buffet of drugs and liquor. You will loosen up and celebrate by having sex. Low self-esteem is your admission to the greatest party on this ship."

Rainbow stopped to listen intently to every word. My heart was racing, my wings were drooping like a flower without water and my feather coat was losing its feathers from the stress. I stood in front of Rainbow and started to blow his hair in his eyes so it would block his vision and buy me some time to whisper my directions to him.

"Is the steward concerned for your future? Is he going to be in your life forever, like your family and me?" I pleaded. "Is this steward going to lead you to the first-class section of the ship, or is he actually going to take you down a dark hole to be with the rats in the stowaway section?" I hoped Rainbow could hear me.

Rainbow was mesmerized by all the beautiful, seductive, white 'cats,' the young women that were swaying from side to side, looking for attention. I saw him lick his lips as they batted their eyelashes. I needed to distract him— if I could only fly I would circle the ship and cause a fury that would make everyone run for cover.

"God why can't I fly?" I screamed in anguish. Suddenly a little mouse ran up the mast and away from me. I knew God heard me, but still I couldn't fly.

I tried to turn Rainbow around but he still wouldn't move, so I jumped in front of him. "I want you to look very carefully at the steward's face and think about what you see."

Rainbow and I watched as a family of skunks walked toward the steward. "Don't get too close to them, or you'll get sprayed. It's the skunk's way of protecting himself against danger, a defense mechanism that helps him say NO!"

Then there were the spotted owls, which approached the steward in pairs of two. They like to sleep all day, but together they are up all night. "We mate for life and only look for a new mate in very special circumstances," said the owls to the steward. "We won't be going to the party!"

Suddenly a family of rabbits hopped toward the steward and took their ticket from his hands, heading straight for the party. "We love going down our holes and have sex from morning to night. That is why we multiply."

When Rainbow approached the steward and looked into his face he yelled out, "You're a rat! I will not accept an invitation to your party," and he walked away.

This time I jumped so high for joy that I banged my head against the mast. "I wish I had made that decision when I was young," I said to myself as I bowed my bumped head in shame. I learned from watching over Rainbow that addiction weaves you into her web of deception through the different disguises she wears, such as a 'friend' with the boy-next-door look to a popular girl on the cheer-leading squad. She will tempt you to make the wrong choice. If you make a poor decision, it will cause you to live as a stowaway on your ship. You'll drift among the waves, not knowing in which direction you are headed. Rainbow had learned to say "NO" to temptation.

Delighted with his self-control, Rainbow headed down the gangway of the ship. "The best way I can fight off temptation is to remember what values I live by." He sat on a bench and started to reflect. I whispered gently in his heart, which was now as calm as the ocean.

"You're already cool. You're already sailing in the first-class section of this ship. You don't need to follow the crowd because you're comfortable with who you are. Your body is the temple that holds your soul. Your temple will not be damaged, defaced or treated disrespectfully."

Then I heard Rainbow say, "I respect myself."

After Rainbow weathered his emotional storm, he saw a light shimmering like a beacon in the distance, calling to him with love. It reminded him that his family was waiting at home for him with open arms.

"Follow the light and don't give up," I reassured him. "You'll know you've reached land when a parrot will fly to you to tell you, "Land ahoy! You've arrived safe and sound!"

As the anchor plunged into the ocean, I turned to him and asked, "Do you realize that you were always the captain of your own ship? It was your journey all along. You made the right choice that kept you safely on course. BRAVO!"

CHAPTER ELEVEN

Rainbow Feels Deserted

*R*ainbow stood for a moment looking up at the mountain in the center of the island where he just landed. As he reflected about the months behind him, he started to learn that there are no endings to a person's journey, just beginnings. He knelt down and said a prayer of gratitude for coming this far. He was a young man who battled many obstacles in search of his dream and I could feel he was getting closer to it, if he kept in touch with his heart where he could hear me speak words of wisdom.

"What is your dream?" I asked Rainbow, who was now more open to my voice speaking through his heart. "Do you want to be a teacher, a police officer or a hockey player? Whatever your dream, Rainbow, it will take lots of hard work, discipline and focus on the mountain peak above to make your dream a reality.

"Look up and imagine that the mountain is wrapped with a rainbow that starts right at your feet. Chase the rainbow one step at a time until you reach the pot of gold where your dream is held, full of richness and life. If you don't follow the rainbow and choose another route, you'll only find a pot of broken stones because you didn't want to work hard at making your dream come true." I could see him absorbing my words.

"If you procrastinate putting off today what you think you can do tomorrow, you will only create a barren desert to cross," I continued to tell him to prepare himself for his next climb. "To climb the mountain of your dreams, education will take you to places higher than drugs and alcohol can ever reach." Rainbow got up and started to walk mumbling. "Why? I hate high school. It's so boring," he sounded impatient.

"Education is one of the necessary tools you'll need in order to make your dream come true. Just like a mountain climber who physically increases his strength in order to reach the top of his mountain, education will strengthen your mind."

"How does education strengthen my mind?"

"You're expanding your knowledge for learning. If a mountaineer gets lazy, his muscles get weaker and he can't climb. Before you know it, he'll lose everything he's worked so hard for," I said, hoping he'd understand the parallel I was trying to make.

As Rainbow turned around the bend in the road he suddenly came upon a desert that appeared out of nowhere. He couldn't believe what he saw as he started to cross the ripples of sand that blew so softly with the wind. As he walked, his endurance had weakened because he hadn't been schooled enough or had a thirst for learning. The only way he could ever get across the flat barren land would be through education, but he kept falling down because of the intense heat.

The heat represented the pressure he received from teachers, parents, coworkers and coaches when he wasn't working hard enough. Choosing a life of partying and watching TV instead over doing homework and studying would only lead to broken dreams and make the desert crossing even harder.

Rainbow saw a scorpion hiding under a rock and a snake sliding into a hole. "They're like people who can't get the right job. They are uneducated and can only work in low-income jobs," I whispered to him.

Suddenly a mirage appeared and an armadillo moved slowly toward it. I watched this stubborn creature head in its direction, believing that his way is always the right way. I felt my wings shaking and my coat losing another feather as I recalled running into mirages with all the strength I could muster up, only to find that they disappeared before my eyes. Rainbow found it difficult to turn his back on this mirage, which showed a picture of a future destination where everything came easy with little or no effort—in essence, an easier route than climbing a mountain to reach your dream. "It's a mirage, Rainbow. Don't get tricked into this imaginary vision," I told Rainbow as he started to run quickly toward it.

My wings flapped as I jumped up and down, creating ripples in the sand. I yelled, "When you waste your dream by taking the wrong path, the tumbleweed will come rolling by and carry your dream away. You'll be lost in the desert of life. The scorching sun will diminish your knowledge and the buzzards will wait to pick you apart. Think of the buzzards as failure—getting fired from a job, repeating a grade, losing credits, or getting kicked off a sports team.

"Ask yourself, Rainbow, what consequences lay ahead for you without an education? Think about how education can direct you toward your dream. Education and hard work are the keys to making your dream come true. Quenching your thirst for knowledge will help you get across the desert.

"You can do it! A life without a dream is no life at all."

CHAPTER TWELVE

Beware of Falling Rocks

Rainbow heeded my advice and started to take a path away from the desert of false dreams. He studied hard in school, listened to his teachers until he finally graduated from high school. Rainbow had crossed his personal desert of life.

High school took its toll on Rainbow, however. He was tired from all the hard work, and still wasn't sure of what he wanted to do or where he wanted to go. He took some time off to relax and I stayed right beside him, hoping he would search in his heart for the answers to his questions about his future.

Then one day, as he sat down in a meditative posture, I heard him ask me from deep in his heart. "If I get tired of the same path can I change direction as long as it is the right one?" He hummed to the universe.

"Quite often when something doesn't work to your advantage, it means you were not meant to remain on that path. It is time for a change," I replied with reassurance. "We are always coming to a crossroads in life. You can be 70 years old and still be confused about which way to go. That's why you need to sit like you are sitting and go inside yourself to get the answers."

After meditating, Rainbow got up with renewed energy and said goodbye to the path that had gotten him this far. He began his new journey on a path that hopefully would lead him to his dream. As he walked up his mountain, he gazed at the stars against the night sky and felt the cool breeze luring him toward his destination. Little did he realize that the older he got the more difficult, and rewarding, life became!

෧෩෩෧

Rainbow had just entered university and he was the talk of the campus. With broad shoulders and a great physique, he dominated the sports field as the star quarterback of the football team. I ran with him as he dodged the linebackers. At the championship game, it was his final 40-yard pass that scored the winning touchdown with nine seconds left in the game. The girls were as crazy about him as I was.

He worked hard to stay on the straight and narrow. He limited his appearance on the party circuit and avoided alcohol and drugs. He often studied at night while I sat on the edge of his bed and listened to him cursing about a 'foreign' subject he was trying to master.

"I hate economics," he would mutter under his breath.

I watched Rainbow lie on his bed staring at the ceiling and worrying about the final exams coming up. He knew that if he didn't make the grade he would be kicked off the football team.

His dad came into his room with a cup of hot chocolate and sat down on top of me where I was sitting. "I had trouble with math when I was in university. I almost gave up," he told Rainbow.

"Why didn't you?" said Rainbow. "I wanted so much to be an architect and I couldn't if I didn't have my math."

"So how did you manage learning it?" Rainbow looked up with eyes filled with frustration. "I took a break, had a hot chocolate with my dad and got some help from him." Rainbow was relieved to hear his dad's offer of help. "Don't be afraid of it," said his father. "Embrace the learning experience."

"Stop worrying about things you can't control," I added to reassure him further. "Study hard and I know you will do your best." But he didn't hear me, this time because he was too busy working through math problems with his dad.

I knew that everything happens for a reason. It's no different than a mountain climber who concentrates carefully to take one step at a time. He doesn't want to disturb any loose rocks and lose his balance. The mountain climber has no time to worry about what could happen to him as he pushes carefully upward. He has the confidence to climb and knows he can't control the weather conditions that lie ahead, just like Rainbow can't control tomorrow's exams.

After Rainbow's dad had left the room, Rainbow put his pencil down and stopped working. I knew something was bothering him. I listened inside his thoughts to see where his emotions were headed. Rainbow was feeling guilty about the mistakes he made in the past.

"Being guilty is only going to weigh you down. There is nothing you can do about it!" I yelled from across the room while I was trying to practice my flying. I fell and knocked off the glass of water on his table. He picked it up.

"I moved it." I yelled! "If I can't fly maybe I can knock things around," I said to myself. After all these years I realized I was trying so hard to fly that if I just relaxed and practiced what I preached I could move mountains, too.

Suddenly a gust of wind smacked a tree branch outside against his bedroom window, as if it was applauding me. I knew that God was giving me his sign of approval.

Rainbow was trying to deal with the remorse for the bad times in his life. He was especially weighed down by the time he had wasted when he was drinking and doing drugs with the coyotes.

"The guilt will create black rocks in your invisible knapsack. Guilt can eat away at your dreams, like termites slowly feeding on the foundation of a house," I said, sitting next to him at his desk.

"Once you make a mistake, such as stealing or hurting someone's feelings, it's hard to undo what you've done. Making amends is important. Returning the money you stole shows you're sorry for your behavior. However, an apology only works if you really mean it from the deepest part of your heart.

"Even when we make amends, we still feel very guilty for what we have done, especially if the person we've hurt does not forgive us. But, it's important to forgive yourself and every enemy that has broken your heart. This way you will find closure in every relationship that has disappeared with the wind," I continued. Rainbow was deep in prayer and I knew he was hearing me through the passageway of his heart.

"If you bury your problems deep within your soul, you have only fooled yourself; you'll only hide your problems, and they'll become like parasites slowly eating away your insides. And the daring journey to becoming your true self will only become weakened."

CHAPTER THIRTEEN

Embracing the Path of the Unknown

A couple of years went by and we were still climbing up Rainbow's mountain. I was constantly reminding him not to be afraid to continue climbing the twisted, rugged road that wrapped its way around. At every turn we entered the unknown and at every turn he continued to grow, allowing himself to embrace what crossed his path. He was still working hard to make his grades and keep active in sport activities. And he continued to keep close ties with his loving family and friends.

One day, I remember vividly entering a path that was lined with colorful black-eyed Susans dancing around tree trunks in a meadow of hay that went on for acres. On this path there were certain animals that made their home— including a rooster, a peacock and a horse.

Rainbow approached the red rooster, introduced himself and asked him what he did for a living.

"I'm Entitlement," said the red rooster. "I have the privilege to announce the sun waking up in the morning and I don't have to do anything all day long because I'm the red rooster. I don't have to earn my privileges because they are handed to me. I strut proudly. Whatever I want in the barnyard I get and that is why I don't need to go up to the top of any mountain to fulfill my dream. I expect my dream to come to me. That is why I am entitlement."

Rainbow then turned to the next animal to cross his path, the peacock. "Who are you and what do you do for a living?"

"My name is Conceit," said the peacock. "I'm vain and full of myself. I'm the most beautiful creature that you will ever meet in the meadow of hay. I look down on everyone, as they could never inherit such beauty. I walk up and down this path of golden straw and watch how everyone stops and looks at me in admiration. They are all envious of my feathers. I open them up like a fan and then I walk away as I will not have anything to do with others. They are not worthy of my presence.

"I'm not beautiful on the inside and I don't care, because nobody is going to see my inside. Besides, it's my outside beauty that really counts. I often sit at my vanity table looking into my mirror and know that there will never be another me."

Rainbow then greeted the horse on his path upward.

"I'm Diligence," said the horse. "I believe in working hard to achieve my dream. When I get tired, I stop, sit down, rest and think about what I should do next. Then I start all over again, one step at a time, pushing and pulling my wagon up to the top of the mountain. I'm gentle, even when things go wrong along my path and the load that I'm carrying becomes too heavy. I don't give up. After a brief rest, I have the inner strength to gallop into the wind toward the sunset. I'm grateful for the life I have been given."

Rainbow said goodbye to the animals and continued on his journey. He still had quite a trek up his exhausting and challenging mountain. He started to contemplate which of these animals related best to him. He was reminded of making the right choice in life and knew that he wanted to be like the horse, working diligently to make his dream come true.

He was starting to develop patience and wisdom. He sat and waited for his endurance to build, like the mountaineers who rest before taking the next step and assess their next move before continuing with their climb.

He was preparing for his next phase in life. He understood that you never know what surprises lurk behind every corner!

CHAPTER FOURTEEN

Beware the Road of Thorns

"Not this again!" I complained to God. "Why do I have to relive this nightmare all over again?" The sky began to darken and the thunder rolled across it. It was his way, I thought, of telling me that one more strike and I'd be out if I kept swearing at him. "Remember, Autumn, I have a plan," God said to me, his voice very loud and clear. "You keep questioning my motive—why can't you fly, why can't he see you. Remember what I told you in the beginning. Have trust in my plan and stop complaining. You're not the only angel without wings."

Rainbow had just arrived at the point on the mountain I dreaded most—the Land of the Seven Deadly Masks. It blocked his entrance to the Road of Thorns, which eventually leads him to the top of the mountain peak. Sensing the rough environment, Rainbow looked inside himself for strength through this final hurdle.

I told him that this was going to be one of his toughest challenges. "There are masks that will frighten and test you. You will quickly put up walls, creating your very own fortress around you. Within seconds, your heart will start to harden. Don't be afraid, Rainbow. Remember to pray. You have your personal values you hold dear to your heart and the recipe for that special birthday cake if you need it. These tools are your protective armour against temptation and the thorns that line the road where the masks make their home," I told him.

"If you address the fear that is holding you prisoner within your own soul, the masks will weaken as they try to crash through your fortress to break you down. The masks are after your values, preventing you to get to the top of your mountain peak. The way to succeed at battle with them is to remember how important your life is to you. Cut the branches of thorns one day at a time."

I watched Rainbow as he moved his way carefully through the vines of thorns. As he took a sword to cut the first branch in front of him he came face to face with the first mask, the Mask of Envy. With glee in its eyes, the mask faced Rainbow with piercing eyes. The Mask of Envy wears jealousy on his face and has envy for Rainbow's self-respect.

"Rainbow, don't get involved with this mask and become jealous of what others have. If you do, the Mask of Envy will become a part of you and you will become envious of what you can't have—someone else's life," I warned him.

"The only way to win the battle with the Mask of Envy is to be grateful for everything that God has sent your way. Being grateful turns negative energy into positive energy. When you show appreciation, the Mask of Envy melts away."

Rainbow was listening to me as he turned the other direction and continued through the road made of thorns. He moved forward and cut the twisted branches in front of him, but his frustration was building when the deadly Mask of Anger appeared.

"Watch out, Rainbow! This mask has the strength to destroy you, if you let it. This is the one mask that wears many faces." The mask was blazing with fire created from the anger that it held inside. "Watch your back. This mask will turn into violence, as his strong emotions can grow and burn out of control.

"To prevent this mask from becoming your new friend, you must defuse any anger that you hold inside by exploring where your anger is coming from. Once you explore the route it has taken and funnel it into something positive, the Mask of Anger will change to the Mask of Calmness. You can then stand up to it and look directly in its eye, and it will disappear."

Rainbow positioned himself cross-legged, rested his hands on his knees and meditated to find peace and forgiveness in his heart for himself and others.

Rainbow was now feeling more confident after having battled two of the masks. He continued to cut his way through the thicket of thorny branches. As he moved up the dark road where thorns pricked the bottom of his feet until they bled, he met the Mask of Pride, who was hanging from the tree in front of him.

"I will not let you through," said the Mask of Pride to Rainbow. "Nor will I allow myself to bend in any way. I will stand guard in this position and refuse to let anyone through."

Rainbow wasn't sure what to do. He stopped to contemplate his next move. "Look at this mask carefully and you will see that it's his vanity that blocks this mask from moving forward," I told him. "If you become just as stubborn as him, refusing to bend in certain situations, you will block the entrance to your soul, preventing you from having access to your true self. You'll have false pride if you insist on taking this mask on. You will never say you're sorry for the injustice and injury you have shown toward others. Through your false pride you will never develop your personal growth.

"Take the high road," I encouraged him. "If you understand someone's faults and have compassion for them, you won't become stubborn and angry." Rainbow took my advice and took another route through the Land of the Seven Deadly Masks.

The other road of thorns proved to be even more difficult, as he cut, chopped and walked over thorns after thorns, his feet full of cuts and aching with pain. Then he noticed from each thorn came a bud. As he walked past them, the buds grew and blossomed into the most beautiful red roses he had ever seen. He started to pick the roses one by one until he met the deadly Mask of Gluttony.

The mask approached Rainbow with baskets filled with roses of all different colors, scents and textures. "You must be tired from all the thorns. I offer to you all these beautiful fragranced florals to heal your discomfort while traveling the road of thorns. When you smell these roses, their sweet fragrance will keep you coming back for more until eternity," said the Mask of Gluttony.

"Rainbow," I whispered. "The roses can't ever satisfy you once you let the Mask of Gluttony take control of you. Overindulgence will spoil and decay your soul. It's like having a birthday party every day; too many presents leave you with no sense of appreciation. Too much cake and ice cream make your teeth fall out and you'll explode from overeating! To do battle with the Mask of Gluttony, you must wear the armour of knowing when enough is enough!"

Rainbow did this by remembering what he learned when he went into treatment—eating healthy, staying in touch with friends and giving himself some time to relax. He also maintained his physique by exercising at the gym and practicing to throw a football.

Many days had passed and Rainbow kept chopping away the thorny branches, which kept growing and growing taller, by remembering all that he had learned throughout his life journey. His task was easier when he reflected and recited the serenity prayer.

One day when he raised his arm to cut a very thick branch in his way, he heard a scream. "Don't you dare touch me. I am the deadly Mask of Greed. I'm going to break through the windows of your fortress by stealing your values and teaching you not to share what you have with others."

Again, I offered Rainbow some perspective on this mask's pitfalls. "The only way to battle greed is to hold on tight to your personal values and share your material possessions with those in need. In other words, don't fill your pockets and empty your soul. Instead, give to others who are less fortunate."

As much as Rainbow worked hard to get through this difficult period, I could see it was weighing him down and he was ready to give up. In fact, he was growing so tired that all he wanted to do was rest and not work anymore. While he lay there doing nothing, the earth moved from under him and lifted him up as the ground split in two.

"I am the deadly Mask of Sloth," said the ground beneath him. "I don't move or work. I lie here on this ground made of mud and rocks. This is my place! Go somewhere else to lie down." Rainbow focused on the mask as he spoke and saw that he resembled a pig. "I'm greedy and

I don't share my food with the other masks. I do nothing but eat all day long. I have no energy to pursue my dreams. And if you take one step forward I will devour you in one slurp and take you with me to live below the earth."

The Mask of Sloth looked at Rainbow with eyes as blank as a TV screen turned to static. "Rainbow, if you get sucked into watching this hypnotic mask, you will be blinded from seeing the entrance to your dream. The only way you can rid yourself of this mask is to focus on the horizon and the impending sunset, like the horse that rides into the sunset. Remember your values are like the workhorse that hauls and ploughs through tough jobs to make dreams come true. Take one step in front of another until you gain energy and endurance."

Rainbow shook his head to break the Mask of Sloth's gaze and started to work hard like the horse to get through the Land of the Seven Deadly Masks and head to the top of his mountain peak. He was weak, tired and thirsty from being on the road for so long. But the more vines he cut, the more light that began to shine through and the closer he got to the end of his struggle. Soon he would be released from the grip of thorns that had held him for so long. As he said his serenity prayer, he took one final swoop with his sword, and found himself at the end of the Road of Thorns.

In front of him was a yellow house with a white picket fence. The sign on the door said "Welcome" and Rainbow entered, looking for relief. In the living room was a mask that looked innocent and pure, like children in a schoolyard, but it disguised its evil temptations. The house lured the innocent into its domain, then its inhabitant, the Mask of Lust, showered its guests with gifts and compliments, only to prey upon them when they least expect it and rape them of their innocence.

I warned Rainbow of this mask's evil: "The only way to confront this abuser is to scream out loud and let the world know the threat of fear that lives inside the yellow house with the white picket fence. Never enter a house unless you know who lives inside or trust a stranger to 'worship' your body. Refusing the Mask of Lust's presents and charm means refusing the entrance to his dungeon.

"If anyone attempts to abuse you, hurt you or strip you of your dignity, don't be afraid to get help. Call the police to bring these torments to an end."

Rainbow ran from the yellow house to get help. As he looked back, he saw a flock of hawks from the forest fly down, pick apart the rooftop, then the interior and destroy the yellow house and the Mask of Lust inside.

I was proud of Rainbow for his accomplishments and for the young man he grew up to be. He had come face to face with the Seven Deadly Masks and won the battle of their temptations, becoming a person of great power, wealth and dignity. His invisible knapsack was now filled with more values, all of which he had earned over the years.

I shed a tear as I recalled how I didn't have the same confidence when I arrived at the Land of the Seven Deadly Masks. My self-esteem was so low that I didn't have the strength or the willpower to overcome the battle I was facing.

As Rainbow and I continued walking forward, I looked back and could see an image of myself, as a young woman being hugged by my Summer. She was whispering to me, telling me that I was not a bad person and that I still had a chance to change my behavior.

"You can fix this," I remember her saying to me. "Don't be afraid. We all make mistakes and through our mistakes we learn our greatest lessons in life. Some battles are won and some are lost. We are the only ones who can hold ourselves back from making our dreams come true."

I turned and followed Rainbow up the final stretch on his personal mountain.

CHAPTER FIFTEEN

Rainbow's Final Push to the Top

*R*ainbow was now getting closer to the top of his magical mountain and the end of his journey. He followed the snow-covered trails that led him to two tall iron gates just beyond the clouds.

A pair of white saber-toothed tigers guarded the iron gates. And beyond the gates was the City of Doors. Rainbow was standing at the gates, eagerly waiting to be congratulated by his professor as he graduated from university. His best friend, Alder, was right behind him in his graduation robe giving Rainbow a pat on the back. In the audience were his parents and the rest of his extended family with tears of joy and pride as they celebrated Rainbow's graduation into a new phase of life.

"This is where you'll be tested on everything you've learned so far," I said to him. "This is no different than university, where you must take your exams to see if you can graduate to the next level. If you didn't study, didn't care or had a bad attitude, then you would be in danger. The tigers are like your teachers and they'll know by your answers if you've learned anything throughout your entire journey."

The tigers paced slowly around Rainbow, smelling his scent. They sensed the emotions that sat inside his soul. As they were circling him, I explained to him that the tigers were looking for a certain number of characteristics before they let him go any further. "Are you weak, or are you strong? Are you confident to go through the iron gates to the City of Doors? Have you made the emotional transformation from angry to peaceful? Have you used your curiosity to explore? Have you found the secret to becoming the person you are meant to be? Did you learn from every failure that you've encountered? Did your courage help you to challenge yourself and not miss any opportunity that life has presented?

"Rainbow, the tigers can sense where you have come from. They know if you are ready for the opportunity that awaits you behind the iron gates. If they sense you're not ready, they will not let you in to discover the City of Doors."

I encouraged Rainbow to introduce himself to the tigers.

"My name is Honor," growled one of the tigers.

"I'm Respect," the second tiger said, showing his teeth that were made of ivory to match his coat of snow white.

"Why are you here guarding the iron gates to the entrance of the City of Doors?" Rainbow asked.

"We guard the gates to the City of Doors that lead you to the Land of Fulfillment," said Honor. "No one enters unless they have the dedication and passion to stay on the right path in life. They must show us that they have no fear, holding their heads up high in search of their dream. Just because someone has opportunity it doesn't mean they'll use it wisely.

"This Land of Fulfillment is where the journey really begins. The doors of all shapes and sizes represent everything you have worked toward to make your dream come true. Once the doors are opened, the possibilities are revealed; possibilities of what you can become when you work hard and believe in yourself and hold the values that are dear and close to your heart. It is the Land of Fulfillment that will redirect your life and help you go after new dreams and rediscover your full potential."

The white tiger moved slowly around Rainbow as he spoke to him.

"We cannot be fooled," said Respect. "We can see right through you with our jeweled eyes."

Rainbow bent down to kneel before them. "I'm worthy of entering the City of Doors," he said sincerely. "I have a dream that I carry in my golden locket, which is valued with respect and love. I have been true to myself. I have made mistakes along the way, but I also took responsibility for those mistakes. I also know that every night after a hard day's work or when I wake up in the morning, I can look at myself in the mirror and see my reflection.

"I know my shortcomings and my strengths. I know whether or not I have a face of honesty or a face of deception. It is in my heart that I can always depend on myself and not anyone else to make my dream come true. I learned that if I don't take the time to pray or meditate to seek guidance I will not hear the answer I'm searching for," Rainbow continued with more self-assurance than I'd ever heard in him.

"I want to be a powerful mountain climber that is not afraid to take the giant climb upward to make my dreams take flight. I dream so many dreams of what I want to become. I thought of becoming a police officer—keeping the peace and helping others to be safe. Or a doctor— finding cures to save people's lives. Maybe even a teacher, who inspires students with a thirst for learning or a poet that will always be remembered forever with a message of hope.

"However, regardless of what I want to be, I know that more than anything, I must dedicate myself to keeping my dream alive. And to get there, I know there are no shortcuts in life. I will always be presented with new challenges until the day I die. It's at these crossroads that the choice will always be mine. Should you open the iron gates that protect the City of Doors I promise not to waste my dream, like the small man who lives in the house made of jewels that I met on my journey.

"I will not be lazy like the pig that I also met along the way; I will not feel a sense of entitlement like the rooster, who believed that his dream would be handed to him. Instead, I will work hard like the horse, and I will remember that I'm the captain of my ship.

"I realize that this is *one* of the most important days of my life as I have to make a choice to take one step at a time and continue my recovery from my addictions. When I'm in trouble, I will use the wizard's recipe to make my cake of sobriety. I will not put off until tomorrow what I must do today, letting my dream blow away like the tumbleweeds I saw in the desert."

I was so proud of Rainbow, as he stood tall with great confidence. Before I could whisper my praise to him, Rainbow asked the tigers if they thought he was worthy of walking through the gates into the City of Doors. "If not," he said to them, "I'm willing to work harder to earn the privilege."

Rainbow spoke with truth in his voice. And the tigers sensed it. The white tigers stood up tall and led Rainbow to the iron gates to let him through. The city was filled with thousands of doors. Some were so tall that they required a ladder to reach their doorknobs, while others were so small that they were easily overlooked. Each one had a different doorknob, requiring a certain talent to open it in order to be led to the Land of Opportunity. ·

"Each of these magical doors has the name of a person on it," said Honor, turning to Rainbow.

"If you look closely you will see a door that is made of quilts. This is for a particular child who wants to design quilts of all different colors when he grows up. Another is made with paintbrushes awaiting for the arrival of an artist," added Respect.

"The door with the musical notes is for a musician who will create his own symphony. The door with books on it is for the writer to discover, " said Honor, swishing his tail back and forth as if he were conducting an orchestra.

"There are many doors made of red crosses for a person who will be a healer, as well as a door that is covered in stars for an astronomer in search of the mysteries of the universe," said Respect.

"The small door is for the person with the gentle heart that will care for animals who need help." Honor bowed his head with pride.

"The tallest door, where you can't see the doorknob, is waiting for a special person who will bring peace to the world," added the other tiger. "That is the hardest door to open. Yet, if only people would understand and make the right choice, the door simply requires a tall ladder in order to open it."

"What street is my door on?" Rainbow asked the tigers.

"Your door is the door with the dream you chose for yourself," said Honor. "It has been waiting here for you to arrive."

As the tigers lead him down the winding road of doors, they bring him to the Street of Curiosity. Rainbow sees his door.

Respect stood up on his hind legs to direct Rainbow to his door. It was tall and painted in rainbow colors. "Your name is there!" He moved in closer to Rainbow. "All you have to do is open it and go inside to the Land of Opportunity."

Before Rainbow approached the door, he asked the tigers, "What if someone doesn't know what their dream is? Does that mean there is no door with their name on it?"

"There are a lot of people who have trouble finding what their dream is. For some it takes a long time, others know it right away. This does not mean that there isn't a door with their name on it waiting for them. Once you open a door and go inside and you do not know what your dream is yet, you will see a long hallway that will guide you to where you need to be. Being true to yourself, being comfortable with who you are, and just growing up to be a kind person is, in itself, a dream come true."

"Thank you so much for bringing me here. I'm so very grateful to you both for leading me to my final destination."

"This is not your final destination, it is just the beginning of what lies ahead for you when you dare to dream!" said Honor, roaring to make his point heard.

Just before Rainbow walked through his door, Respect asked him, "Don't you recognize us?"

"We are the two little kittens that you met at the beginning of your journey: Innocent and Dream," said

Honor, who went on to explain how they earned their new names and roles.

"We followed our dream with hope and faith in our hearts, remaining pure in our desire to be on the right path, and now we are mightier than all the animals in the forest," added Respect.

"It's because of our strength to stay on the right path that we have been chosen to lead you to your door," Honor told Rainbow. "Now turn the knob and go inside."

The tigers stood back to give Rainbow room. As he turned away from Respect and Honor, I watched him slowly and carefully turn the knob. The door opened quietly and Rainbow turned around to say his final good-byes but the tigers were already gone. Ahead of him lay the Land of Opportunity. It was filled with even more experiences that Rainbow would learn from.

I was never as proud as I was at this moment, watching my Rainbow graduate from university. We were floating on a cloud of happiness as I escorted him up to receive his degree on stage.

കൗപ്

In the months that followed, he took his place at the top of his magical mountain where there was a cloud in the shape of a desk. He took his position behind the desk, and sat on the chair shaped like an apple. He looked back to see the long and winding road we traveled to get here.

"What do you see? Look carefully," I whispered.

Rainbow saw me, his angel flying through the window of the hospital with his golden locket that held his special dream. I watched him reach into his heart and pull out his locket. Rainbow opened it to uncover his special dream—he had graduated to become a teacher.

He looked up and said, "Autumn, I can see and hear you, don't you remember me?"

I was puzzled, and then I moved closer and took my hand to move my long silver hair that fell in front of my face. I looked straight into Rainbow's eyes and saw Summer, staring back at me. Summer had reincarnated into Rainbow, who was now taking me on this journey to travel the same route and relive my life one step at a time, and teaching me that we must not waste the dream we are given by God.

I never was the teacher. I was the lost soul that needed to earn my wings before I could fly. Rainbow was my brave teacher who helped me to realize that your wildest dreams can come true if you have faith in yourself and the will to succeed and stay on the right course.

This was my graduation too—a graduation of compassion and forgiveness for my previous life that I had wasted. In the near distance, two clouds in the shape of giant hands applauded me on my graduation. It was God smiling down on me.

I looked up at the majestic sky above me and for the first time could spread my wings like an eagle. "Yahoo! I can fly." My echo bounced like a jumping bean around the universe for all the other angels to hear.

Then Rainbow opened up his heart and a bright light poured out. From the light, Summer stepped out. She was as beautiful as the first time I saw her, when she came to visit me as a baby in the nursery many years ago.

With tears of joy in our eyes, we joined hands and took our first steps together as angels side by side. We both lifted our wings to return back to God, and with all the power we could muster, we yelled,

"Let our dreams take flight!"

Check your local bookstore or retailer for Diane Dupuy's books or order here.
Just fill out the form below and send it, along with your payment, to:

BEYOND BLACKLIGHT INC.
33 Lisgar St., Toronto, ON M6J 3T3
Or fax or phone us at: **Fax: 416-532-6945 • Telephone: 416-532-1137**

Diane Dupuy will be more than happy to personally sign each book upon request.

Ask about discount orders on quantity purchases. For orders of 5 to 10 books, we'll pay the shipping costs and throw in a free copy! Diane Dupuy's other publications are also available: *Daring to Dream, Throw Your Heart Over the Fence* and *The Little Girl Who Did What?!!!*

Please send me:

_____ copies of **The Teacher and the Soul**   @ $21.95 CDN ea. _____

_____ copies of **Daring to Dream**   @ $24.95 CDN ea. _____

_____ copies of **Throw Your Heart Over The Fence** @ $26.95 CDN ea. _____

_____ copies of **The Little Girl Who Did What?!!!** @ $14.95 CDN ea. _____

Shipping & Handling $5.00

$1 for each additional book _____

SUBTOTAL _____

Canadian residents add 7% GST _____

TOTAL AMOUNT ENCLOSED _____

Enclosed is my   ☐ Cheque   ☐ Money Order   ☐ Visa   ☐ Mastercard
Please Make Payable To: BEYOND BLACKLIGHT INC.

Card # _____ Expiry date _____ / _____

Signature (Name as on card) _____

Name (Please Print) _____

Address _____

City _____ Province _____

Postal code _____ Phone _____

E-mail address _____ Autographed to: _____